JESSICA BECK

THE DONUT MYSTERIES, BOOK 24

FUGITIVE FILLING

Donut Mystery #24 Fugitive Filling

First Edition: February 2016

The First Time Ever Published!

The 24th Donut Mystery.

Jessica Beck is the *New York Times* Bestselling Author of the Donut Mysteries, the Classic Diner Mysteries, the Ghost Cat Cozy Mysteries, and the Cast Iron Cooking Mysteries.

To P & E,

Always and forever, my reasons why!

When the new attorney in April Springs is found dead soon after a public spat with Jake, Suzanne and her husband must team up to solve the woman's murder before they are both set up to take the fall for a crime neither one committed. Added to the intrigue in her life is news from Suzanne's mother that very well may change the donut maker's life forever.

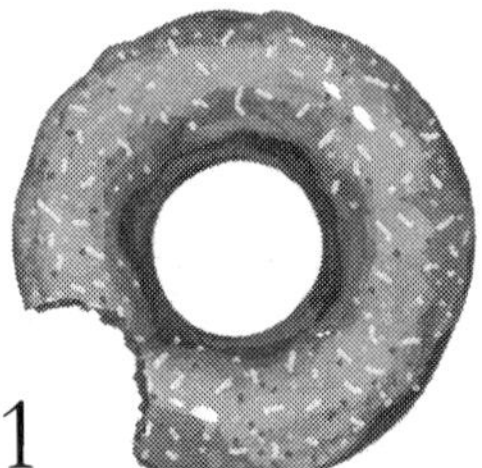

CHAPTER 1

"SUZANNE, IS HE STILL HERE?" my assistant, Emma Blake, asked me as I brought in one of the last trays from the display cases in the front of Donut Hearts.

The "he" in question was Jake Bishop, my husband. Jake had spent most of his career with the North Carolina state police, but after leaving them, he'd reluctantly taken over the reins of the local April Springs law enforcement office as a favor to our friend, the mayor. As acting chief, Jake had been embroiled in a great deal of small-town intrigue, but recently he'd resigned that post as well. Since then, he'd claimed to enjoy his "break" from gainful employment, but I knew my husband. He was getting antsy. Lately he'd begun to come by my donut shop in the morning, grab a coffee and an out-of-town newspaper, and settle in until I got off work.

"He has every right to be," I told Emma. "Jake's worked hard his entire life. He's entitled to a vacation."

"A vacation I understand," young Emma said, "but why aren't you two at the beach where it's warm, instead of here? I just heard the forecast, and in three days we're expecting sleet and freezing rain. That doesn't sound like any vacation I'd like to take."

"Jake may be free, but we have a donut shop to run," I reminded her.

"You know my mother and I would be happy to sub for you any time. Just say the word."

Emma and her mother, Sharon—a sweet woman I sometimes accidently called Cheryl because she reminded me so much of an old college friend I'd once had by that name—took over for me occasionally, and more recently, they were running the donut shop two days a week on a regular basis. It had been difficult for me to give up that much control. I couldn't imagine asking them to step in even more just so I could have a little time off with my husband. Then again, why shouldn't I? Emma was right. Some warm weather might be just what the doctor ordered.

"Thanks. I'll think about it," I said as I walked back up front, leaving Emma with the last of the dishes for the day. I smiled as I grabbed the coffee pot and topped my husband's mug. "Are you sure I can't get you any treats?"

Jake patted his waistline. "Thanks, but I've put on two pounds since I left police work. I've got to watch it, or I won't be able to fit into my pants."

"I wish I had your willpower," I said. Mostly I stayed away from the donuts and other treats that I made, but I had to sample the new recipes, didn't I? Maybe not a whole donut every time, but hey, there were times that you needed to experience the entire thing before you knew for sure whether it was any good or not. At least that's what I always managed to convince myself of. "Emma thinks we need a vacation."

"I'm on one," Jake said as he put the paper aside. "Why would I need another one?"

"She meant one with me. We could always get away to the coast for a little time off," I said. "I hate the thought of you just sitting here every day waiting for me to get off work."

"I didn't realize it bothered you," Jake said with a frown.

As he started to get up, I smiled and put a hand on his shoulder, gently shoving him back down into his seat. "Slow down. Don't go jumping to conclusions. I love having you here. I'm just worried that you're getting bored."

He settled back into his seat. "Suzanne, I risked my life so much on the job that it's actually kind of nice being a little bored."

"So, you admit that you're bored," I said.

"That's not what I meant. I'm just trying to enjoy the absence of stress in my life for a change. I never realized just how much of it I was holding in until it was all gone. If you'd like to take a trip though, I'm on board. Would you like to get away?"

"Not unless you do," I said. "The truth is that I'd rather wait until it starts warming up a little. This is my busiest time of year, but I could easily spare a week in the summer. I doubt April Springs would even notice that I was gone."

"Then let's plan to go somewhere then, assuming that I'm not working again by then."

That surprised me. Jake hadn't said a word about going back to work since he'd resigned as acting chief of police and handing the job over to his second in command, Stephen Grant. Stephen also happened to be the boyfriend of my best friend, Grace Gauge. I know it must sound kind of inbred, but that's what happens in a small town. The cashier at my bank also happened to be married to the grocery store manager, and their daughter worked at the dry cleaner's. Most of our lives touched in some way or another on a daily basis. "What do you think you might like to do?"

"I've been giving it some serious thought, and I might try my hand at opening a donut shop of my own," he said with a grin. "You wouldn't mind a little competition, would you?"

"I had no idea that's what you wanted to do," I answered with a grin of my own as I handed him my keys. "You can have this one, if that's what you want."

Jake held his hands in front of him, refusing to take them. "Okay, you got me. I was bluffing. The truth is, I don't know how you do this every day."

"I take two days off a week now, remember? I used to work all seven."

"How that didn't drive you insane is beyond me," Jake said.

"You didn't answer my question. What else would you like to do?"

"I'm really not sure," he admitted. "That's why I haven't said anything to you about it yet. I know I can't just retire, not at my age. I'm just having a hard time coming up with a new game plan for the rest of my life. Don't worry. Once I do think of something, you'll be the first person I tell."

"I certainly hope so," I said. "Don't rush your decision on my account, though. I kind of like having you around."

"I very much appreciate hearing that. I like being here, too. You don't have to worry about me doing anything rashly. I'm not in any rush. I just thought I should let you know that I'm pondering the situation." Jake frowned for a moment, and then he said, "In the spirit of full disclosure, there's something else I need to talk to you about."

I didn't care for the serious expression on his face. "Go on, I'm listening."

"It can wait until you close for the day," Jake said.

"Cool." I walked over to the sign and flipped it from OPEN to CLOSED. "We are now officially closed for business." Since I didn't have any customers at the moment, it was easy enough to do, and besides, we had less than a dozen donuts left in inventory anyway. "Now talk."

Jake stretched his shoulders a bit as he bit his lower lip, a sure sign to me that he really wasn't ready to talk about whatever was on his mind. "How about if we do discuss it on our walk to the bank? I'd feel better not having to make eye contact with you while I tell you."

"Boy, this is going to be bad, isn't it?" I had a knot growing in my gut the size of a baseball. What was going on?

"It's not good, I'll admit that much, but we can handle it."

His explanation didn't comfort me at all. In fact, I was more concerned now than I had been before. What could be so bad that he didn't want to have to face me to talk about it? "I won't be long."

I boxed the last of the donuts into one container, and then I took the final dirty dishes to Emma. "We're now officially closed."

"We have another fifteen minutes," she protested as she glanced at the clock in the kitchen. "It's not because of something I said, is it?"

"Of course not," I replied, not wanting to get into it with her, mostly because I didn't know what was going on myself. I started imagining several worst-case scenarios, but I had to kill that line of speculation immediately. After all, there was no use borrowing trouble. I'd find out in a few minutes anyway. Forcing myself to keep my mind calm, I ran the reports as I cashed out the drawer in the register. Thank goodness it balanced out. After putting the cash and credit card receipts into the deposit bag, I added the slip and zippered it shut. Sweeping the floor quickly, I turned to find Emma exiting the kitchen. "Do you need any help out here?"

"No, I'm good," I said as I handed her the spare donuts. "Do you have a good home for these?"

"Thanks, I appreciate it. That would be great," she said.

"Then take them with my blessing. I'll see you tomorrow morning."

"You're not working tomorrow, remember?" Emma asked. "You're off for the next two days, unless you want to change the schedule."

"That's right. I remember. I'll see you in three days, then."

She stood close to me and whispered, "Is everything okay?"

"It's fine," I whispered. "Enjoy those donuts."

"Oh, they aren't for me," she answered with a grin.

"Is there by any chance a new young man in your life?"

She grinned. "His name is Chance. I met him in my Econ class."

"Is that really his name?" I asked her.

"So he says," she replied. "See you."

"Bye."

"Later, Jake," Emma added as she exited the building.

My husband offered her a truncated smile. "Bye." Once she'd exited, he asked, "Is she in love again?"

"Emma loves falling in love."

"I hope she doesn't get hurt again," Jake said.

"You sound protective of her."

"I am. Nobody has to tell me how hard it is to find someone in this world to love. I happened to get lucky twice."

It was a sweet thing for him to say, and also a reminder that his first wife, who'd died in a car accident while pregnant with their only child, rarely left his thoughts. I had never tried to compete with her. In fact, I loved hearing the stories Jake told about his life before we met. In a way, getting to know her through him brought the two of us that much closer together. Only now it appeared that something was threatening that.

"Let's go," I said as I turned off the lights and grabbed the deposit bag.

"You didn't have to rush on my account," he said.

"I didn't. I rushed on mine. I'm not at all sure I can take this suspense."

"Suzanne, whatever it is that you're imagining, I can promise you that it's not as bad as you think," Jake said with a frown.

"I'll reserve judgment until I learn what it is that you're so reluctant to tell me," I said. "Hang on a second." I was ninety-nine percent certain that I'd shut off the fryer when I'd made our last donut for the day, but I couldn't take a chance on burning the place down just because I was in a hurry to get out of there.

When I checked, I saw that it was indeed off, as I knew it would be, and everything in back was in perfect order.

It was just too bad that my head and my heart weren't.

"We're all good," I said, and then, in a soft voice, I asked, "Aren't we?"

"Of course we are," Jake said as he hugged me.

Whew. I could barely contain my sigh of relief. Whatever the problem might be, it wasn't with us, and I knew that we could deal with anything else, as long as we were together.

Once we were outside and the front door was locked behind us, I said, "Quit stalling and talk."

"After we stop by the bank," Jake insisted.

"Why do we have to wait until then?"

"Because I know you, Suzanne. Once you hear what I've got to tell you, you're going to forget all about making that deposit."

That would have to be bad indeed. "Are you sure that you still want to tell me?"

"The truth of the matter is that I should have said something to you last night at dinner about what happened, but I wasn't sure if I should, and by the time I decided to bite the bullet and tell you everything, you were already asleep."

"Why did you change your mind?" I asked as I began to walk quickly toward the bank.

"Because I was afraid of how you might react if you heard about it from someone else."

"Me?" I asked, pretending to be surprised by the conclusion he'd jumped to. "Why did you think that? You should know me well enough by now to realize that I'm a levelheaded kind of gal if there ever was one."

Jake didn't even laugh at my attempt at a joke, and I knew that whatever it was, it wasn't going to be just laughed away. I made the deposit as quickly as I could while Jake waited out in the parking lot for me. Once I came back out, I said, "I'm not taking another step until you tell me what's going on."

"Okay. You're right. I can't put this off one second longer. It's about Teresa Logan."

The young attorney had recently taken over the office building I'd inherited from my father. George Morris, the mayor of our fair city, had urged me to do it, and against my better judgment, I'd agreed. It wasn't that Teresa wasn't a good attorney or that I thought she would be a bad tenant. I just didn't want her to have any more interactions with my husband than could be helped. She flirted with him shamelessly whenever she saw him, even if I was standing right there, and I wasn't a fan of her behavior, though I'd seen her do the same thing with other men in town. "What about her?"

"She got a little too familiar with me yesterday afternoon, and I'm afraid that I reacted badly."

I bit my lower lip for a moment before I trusted myself to speak. "What happened?" I wasn't happy to hear that whatever was going on involved Teresa Logan, but I was trying not to overreact until I heard the whole story.

Jake took in a deep breath and then let it out slowly before he spoke. "I was at the bottom of the steps leaving the Boxcar Grill with our dinner last night, and Teresa was on her way in. There's no other way of telling this that's going to make it sound any better than it was, so I'm just going to spit it out. She tried to kiss me, Suzanne."

"She what!" I'm afraid my calm demeanor was now gone. I knew that Teresa had been toying with my husband for several months, but until the night before, she'd never acted on it. "How many times?"

"What are you talking about? That was the first, and the last. I'm afraid I lost my cool, and I started yelling at her to leave me alone, that I was a happily married man. She didn't even look embarrassed when I yelled at her. All she said was, 'If you ever change your mind, you know where to find me. You are a special man, and if you ever get tired of donuts, you should come try some crème brûlée.'"

"Tell me that she didn't really say that," I said, clenching and unclenching my fists.

"Suzanne, I told her that she'd be waiting until we had another ice age, because I was in love with you, and that she'd better knock it off, once and for all. You believe me, don't you?"

"Of course I do," I said as I started marching toward Teresa's law office.

"Do I even need to ask you where you're going?" Jake asked me, resignation heavy in his voice.

"You're the detective. You figure it out," I snapped out, not angry with him but with her. Well, maybe I was a little miffed that my husband hadn't come to me immediately after it had happened, but he clearly hadn't been wrong about my reaction. The young attorney was not only about to be evicted, she was going to get something a great deal more painful than that if I could do it before Jake managed to restrain me.

As Jake caught up with me, my husband asked, "Is there any chance you'll just let this go?"

"That depends. If Max tried to kiss me, would you be willing to just ignore it?"

"Your ex-husband knows better than to ever try that. Besides, he's in love with Emily Hargraves now."

"Just answer the question," I insisted, still determined to get to Teresa as quickly as I could manage it. If my Jeep had been handy, I would have driven there, but the office was closer than my transportation. Besides, I probably couldn't be trusted to drive at the moment. The town of April Springs deserved better than to have me on its streets in this state of agitation. No one would be safe.

"I'd kill him," Jake replied softly.

"Well, don't worry. I'm not planning to commit homicide, but I'm going to come as close to it as I can without actually doing it," I said.

We got to Teresa's office building, and I tried the front door.

It was locked.

"Let me in, Teresa," I said as I banged fiercely on the door. "We need to talk."

There was no reply, but then again, I couldn't blame her. She was probably acting quite prudent keeping something solid between us at the moment.

I had a surprise for her, though. As the landlord, I had a key to the place, and I wasn't afraid to use it.

"Take it easy, Suzanne," my worried husband said as I fumbled with the key.

"Don't get in my way right now, Jake. I'm going to deal with this."

"Just don't do anything you'll regret later," he said. "If I learned one thing in all of my years in law enforcement, it's never hit a lawyer. She'll end up owning Donut Hearts by the time she's through with you if you so much as lay a finger on her."

"I'll keep that in mind," I said as I finally managed to open the building's front door.

"Suzanne," Jake warned me yet again.

I wasn't in any mood to hear it. "Teresa, I'm coming in, whether you like it or not!" Keeping Jake's advice in mind, I added, "This is a surprise inspection of the property. It's allowed in the lease you signed, so I have every right to come in."

Momma had insisted that I use one of her attorneys in Charlotte to draw up the lease, and now I was glad that I had. It had provided me with the perfect excuse to do what I was going to do anyway.

Teresa Logan wasn't in the outer office.

That meant that she must have been cowering in the back area, if she was even in the building at all.

That wasn't going to stop me, though. I was going to search the place from stem to stern, and if she weren't in her office, then I'd find her no matter where she might be hiding.

There wasn't even a lock on her inner office door.

Grabbing the handle, I threw the door open as I shouted, "Teresa Logan, prepare yourself for a world of hurt."

My warning fell on deaf ears, though.

The attorney was there all right, but clearly someone else had gotten to her before I could.

From the look of things, as I took in the body on the floor, I realized that she'd crossed someone else besides me, and it had most likely cost her her life.

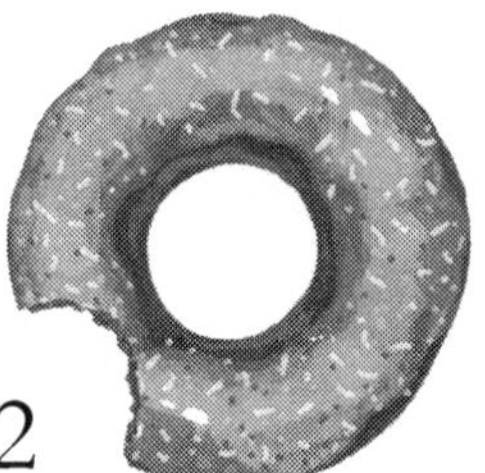

CHAPTER 2

"Is she really dead?" I asked Jake as he leaned over the body and searched for a pulse. Teresa had been dressed for work in a nice suit, and she even still had her shoes on. I knew instinctively that they were expensive, though I didn't recognize them. It was pretty evident that we shopped for clothes in different stores, but I was sure that Grace would immediately recognize the brand.

"I'm afraid so," my husband said as he stood back up. "Suzanne, she's cold to the touch. If I had to guess, I'd say that she was killed sometime last night, but the window's cracked and it feels as though the heat's been turned off in here, so I could be wrong about that."

For some reason, I felt the need to do something, anything, so I went over to close the window when Jake stopped me. "I'm sorry, but you can't do that. This is an active crime scene, so it's important that we don't touch anything."

I nodded. I must have been in shock, trying to do anything as mundane as closing a window. I'd conducted enough investigations of my own to know that, but I wasn't exactly in a good frame of mind at the moment. "What do you think happened to her?"

Jake pointed to what appeared to be a heavy bookend in the shape of a pine cone off to one side of the body. How had I missed that? As I got closer to it, I saw that there were obvious traces of blood and hair on it, and that was when I noticed the blood on the crimson carpet, as well. I'd been planning on changing all of the flooring earlier, but Momma had insisted that cleaning it would be good enough, at least initially. After all, it didn't have to be my taste; it just had to be good enough to satisfy the renter, which it had been.

Jake pulled out his cell phone, and a moment later, he said, "Stephen? This is Jake. You need to get over to Suzanne's building on Viewmont Avenue. There's been a homicide." After a pause, he said, "It's Teresa Logan." He paused for another moment, and then he added, "Yes, I'm sure. You can skip the ambulance and send the wagon instead. She's cold to the touch. We'll be here. Yes, Suzanne is with me. No, we won't."

Jake hung up, but he didn't put his phone away. Instead, he began snapping photos of the body, the murder weapon, and anything else he could see of any interest in the slightest.

"What are you doing?" I asked him. "You realize that you're not a cop anymore, don't you?"

Jake paused taking pictures long enough to frown as he answered me. "Suzanne, at least three people saw me screaming at this woman last night, and today she's dead. I need to dig into this, with or without Stephen Grant's permission. Now, do you want to just stand there, or do you want to help me and start taking pictures with your phone, too? We don't have much time."

"We both need to investigate this murder, not just you," I said as I did what Jake suggested and started taking photos of everything and anything that might be of use to us later.

"I don't want you involved in this. You aren't going to be a suspect," he said.

"You're kidding, right? Everyone in town knows how I feel, felt, about Teresa. You'd better believe my name's going to be on that list right under yours. We both need to figure this out."

"Okay, I get that." Jake punched the button on the attorney's answering machine with the edge of his pen, and we listened as we worked. Two of the messages were pretty mundane, but the last one was chilling. "Do you think you can bully me into settling? It's not going to work, and if you don't back off, you'll be sorry."

"Who was that?" Jake asked me.

The voice sounded vaguely familiar to me, but I wasn't at all sure who it might be. "Play it again."

"Why, did you recognize the voice?"

"Maybe, but I can't put my finger on it. That's not why I want you to replay it, though. I want to record it on my cell phone so I can play it back later."

He hit the play button, and we both remained silent while I recorded the threat on my phone. After it finished playing, Jake asked, "Did you get it?"

"I think so," I said, "but I'm not going to try to figure it out until later. I know we don't have a second to waste right now." I walked over to the desk and found an old-fashioned appointment book sitting on it. Funny, I would have pegged Teresa for someone who kept all of her appointments on her cell phone. It just went to show how little I really knew about the woman. The book was closed, but I wasn't going to let that stop me.

"Don't touch that!" Jake ordered as I leaned over it.

"I wasn't planning to, at least not with my fingers." I pulled a pen out of my pocket to use exactly as Jake had just done earlier. It was the one I'd used to make out the deposit slip, and as I edged it under the front cover, I was glad I had it. My technique was a little awkward, but in twenty seconds, I had the book open to last night's appointments on one side and today's on the other. I took shots of both pages when I heard the first cruiser pull up outside. Jake came over and took a few photos of the entries himself, and then he said, "Wrap it up, Suzanne. We're almost out of time."

I had trouble closing the appointment book, as my pen kept slipping off to one side. I was about to just shut the thing by hand when Stephen Grant burst into the office. Oh, well. I wasn't going to be able to leave everything exactly as I'd found it, but hopefully, that wouldn't matter.

The police chief took one look at the body, then his gaze slid over to the murder weapon, and finally it landed on my husband and me. I was slow putting my phone away, hoping that he didn't suspect what Jake and I had been doing, when he frowned and said, "I need you to wait outside."

"I'd be happy to consult with you on this," Jake offered.

Stephen Grant shook his head. "Thanks, but I'm the chief of police now. If I'm going to prove to the town that the mayor made the right decision, I have to do this on my own."

"I understand completely," Jake said. "Come on, Suzanne."

"We're really not staying?" I asked. No offense to Stephen, but my husband was ten times the police officer Stephen Grant was, and everyone in the room knew it.

"We're really not," Jake said. "Let's let the man do his job."

Once we were out in front of the building, I asked, "Do you really think that he can handle this?"

"I don't really have any choice in the matter, do I? After all, I'm the one who told the mayor he was up to the job," Jake asked after a moment's hesitation. "I think he is, but we're not going to just leave it in his hands. No matter how you cut it, this is going to lead straight back to us; I guarantee it. If we just stand idly by, we could both be in real trouble."

"We have the satisfaction of knowing that we didn't do it, though," I reminded him.

"That will be little consolation if folks start avoiding Donut Hearts because they think one of us is a cold-blooded killer," he said. "Don't take my word for it. You know this town far better than I do. As soon as word gets out that Teresa Logan was murdered, how long do you think it will take most folks to connect it to the two of us?"

"It will be quicker than making bread," I said, knowing that Jake was dead on the money.

"What's that take, three hours?"

I nodded. "About that."

"Then we need to do something to solve this case before that happens," Jake said. "Should we ask Grace to help us, too? I know you two usually work together, and I don't want to butt in on her turf."

My best friend and I had solved a few murders in the past, and it was sweet of my husband to consider her feelings, even during such a troubling time. "There's no need to. She's away on another retreat for business," I said. I'd accompanied her on one the last time she'd gone, and we'd walked right into a buzz saw, so this time, she hadn't even invited me. Not that I could blame her. "She'll be gone all week."

"So then, it's just you and me," Jake said as he nodded.

"The good news is that I've got the next two days off from the donut shop," I reminded him. "It's part of our regular schedule now."

"I know. I had a surprise in store for you before all of this happened."

"What were you going to do?" I asked.

"Not that it matters much now, but I'd been hoping to sneak away to a cabin in the Smoky Mountains for a few days with you," Jake answered.

"That sounds lovely. I'm sorry we won't be going. We'll have to save that for my next break when we're not investigating a murder," I said as the wagon used by the hospital to transport dead bodies showed up, just as some of Stephen's crew arrived on the scene as well. Without exception, every last one of them made it a point to say hello to Jake on their way inside, and more than one nodded at me as well. I knew that my husband had been well loved when he'd been running the police department, and I hoped that Stephen Grant didn't get too much pushback for taking over. Then again, if we were lucky, maybe we'd be able to use that to our advantage in our investigation.

"Do we just stand out here in the cold and wait for him to call us in?" I asked as I rubbed my hands together. It wasn't really that chilly out at the moment, but a cold front was supposed to come through in the next few days, a way for winter to take one final opportunity to stick its tongue out at us before it was done for good. We'd had a relatively mild winter so far, but they were predicting up to half an inch of freezing rain, which had the potential to be deadlier than a foot of snow would be. When that much weight accumulated on power lines and tree limbs, I knew that we were in for a nasty storm, and I hoped they were as wrong as they usually were about our weather. I'd take the snow, or even sleet or just plain rain, but freezing rain was something to fear in our neck of the woods.

"We don't have any choice but to do as he asked us to," Jake said patiently. "You heard the man. There's a great deal of things he and the team have to do before he's going to be free to speak with us. They'll need to get still photos and video of the crime scene, dust for prints, and then inspect the body before they remove it. If I had to guess, I'd say that we'll be here at least another hour, probably longer, before he gets around to us."

"I should have brought coffee," I said, rubbing my hands together, "not that I needed anything to keep me warm on the march over here. I'm sorry Teresa's dead, but I still can't believe that she tried to kiss you."

"Tried, and failed," Jake reminded me. "I'd like to apologize in advance for what you're going to have to put up with because of what happened between the two of us."

"It doesn't matter. You're innocent, and that's all that matters to me," I said. I knew in my heart that my husband hadn't reciprocated Teresa's affection. Max may have cheated on me while we'd been married, but Jake would leave me long before he'd ever dream of doing anything with another woman, and oddly enough, I took a great deal of comfort in that fact.

One of the deputies came out and joined us twenty minutes later. "The chief said that you should both wait for him at his office, Chief." It was confusing sentence structure, but we knew what the officer had meant. "There's no use you two standing out here in the cold." He glanced around and didn't see either of our vehicles. "Do you need a ride?"

"It's five hundred feet away, Rick," Jake said with the hint of a smile. "I think we can both manage it on foot."

"Okay, just checking," the officer replied, and then he saluted Jake with two fingers before he retrieved a kit from the trunk of his squad car.

"Thanks for letting us know," my husband said.

"You bet, Chief."

"I'm not the chief anymore, Rick. You can just call me Jake."

"Sure thing, Chief," Rick replied with a grin. If he was disturbed about the thought that there was a dead body twenty feet away from us, he didn't show it. Then again, Jake wasn't all that shaky either. I, on the other hand, was a bit of a wreck. No matter how many times I managed to stumble across a corpse, it was still very upsetting to me, and I hoped that I never got used to it happening to me.

"You heard the man," Jake said after the officer was gone. "Let's go get out of the cold."

"Does it bother you that he kept calling you Chief?" I asked Jake as we walked over to the nearby police station.

"No, I understand the habit. I've done it myself more than once to former bosses of mine. It kind of goes with the territory."

"You miss it, don't you?" I asked him.

"Parts of it," my husband admitted, "but mostly I'm glad to just sit at home and stoke the fire with you by my side."

"Only I'm not there with you a lot of the time. I'm still working, and I don't plan on shutting the place down anytime soon."

"Then I'll be grateful for every second I get with you," he said with a smile.

"Thank you. That might just be the nicest thing you've ever said to me."

"Oh, I can do better than that, but you'll have to give me a little time to come up with something," Jake said as he took my hand in his and we walked the rest of the way to the police station together. I knew that I'd miss Grace on this investigation, but I also realized with all of my heart that I couldn't have a better partner working alongside me, as long as Jake and I worked out some ground rules first. My husband was used to being in charge, and I didn't have a problem with that per se, but we were going to be equal partners in this investigation, or it wasn't going to work at all. I deserved as much of a voice as he did, and I was going to make sure that he knew that right off the bat, or he and I were going to have a problem. I just had to be sure to do it delicately and bring it up with some subtlety.

"We're equal partners in this, right?" I asked him, instantly abandoning my former strategy and getting it all out on the spot at once. I never was all that good with nuance anyway.

"Of course we are. Why wouldn't we be?" He looked surprised that I'd even asked the question in the first place.

"I just want to be sure we're clear right up front. Jake, I know that you're a great cop, but I bring certain skills to the table myself."

"That's why we're going to make such a good team," my husband answered. "We have complementary skill sets."

"You do look really nice today," I said with a grin.

"Not that kind of compliment," he said.

"I know that, you big dummy," I said as I playfully let go of his hand and smacked his arm. "I just wanted to be sure that you were okay with me contributing to this investigation, too."

"You're kidding, right? Okay with it? Suzanne, I'm counting on it."

"Good. I'm glad that's settled."

As we walked into the police station, Jake nodded to the desk clerk and began to walk past him after he greeted us both.

The man coughed once, and then he said apologetically, "Sorry, Chief, but I need you to sign in on the visitors' book. I hate to ask, but it's policy, you know?"

"Don't worry about it, Darby. It was my policy in the first place, remember?" Jake asked him with a grin as he did as he was told.

"I'm not about to forget it," the cop said. "The chief called and told me that you both can wait in his office. He also said to tell you that he shouldn't be long."

"That's fine. We've got nothing but time at the moment," Jake said as he led me to his former workspace.

"I don't want to be the one who brings this up," I said once Jake and I were alone in his old digs, "but time really is kind of important in our investigation."

"Don't you think I know that?" Jake asked calmly as he studied an old map on the wall that hadn't been there when he'd been in charge. "I know we need to get busy with our own investigation, but we can't let anyone here suspect that we're going to try to solve this case ourselves. We need to keep a low profile as long as we can."

"Jake, you were the police chief not that long ago. How low do you think we can go?"

"You're probably right, but we at least have to try," he said with a sigh. "To be honest with you, I'm not sure how I feel working a case from this side. I'm used to having a badge."

"Don't worry. You'll get used to it, and I'm here to help with the transition."

"That's what I'm counting on."

Less than half an hour later, Stephen Grant came in and joined us. He looked older somehow, as though the weight of his job was pressing heavily upon him. I'd taken a seat, but Jake had been standing behind the desk. He made his apologies as he quickly joined me on the other side. Stephen took it in stride. "You can sit there if you'd like."

"No, sir. I appreciate the offer, but you've got the responsibilities now, so that makes it your seat. I'm more than happy to sit on the other side."

"That's one of the things that I wanted to talk to you about," Stephen said gravely.

"Would you like me to step outside?" I offered.

"No. This concerns you as well, so I'd like you to stay, if you don't mind."

"It's fine with me," I said, trying not to let them both know that I'd just been bluffing. If either man had tried to take me up on my offer to leave, I would have found an excuse to stay put. There was no way that I was going to miss whatever it was the police chief had to say.

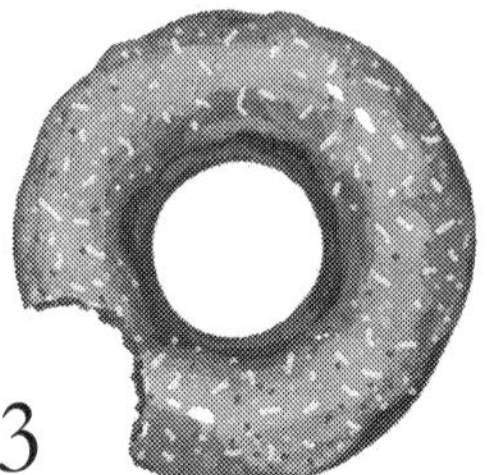

CHAPTER 3

"IS THERE ANY REASON IN particular you two were taking pictures of the crime scene with your phones when I showed up earlier?" Chief Grant asked nonchalantly.

I was about to deny it when Jake said, "I thought it was the prudent thing for us to do. We're going to dig into this case on our own, if that's okay with you."

So much for us keeping a low profile.

"Just because the murder happened in Suzanne's building?" the chief asked his former boss and mentor.

"I'm afraid there's more to it than that. If you haven't heard this news yet, you're going to find out soon enough, so if it's all the same to you, I'd rather you heard from me first."

"I'm listening," he said, folding his fingers into a tent in front of him. He didn't show much reaction, and I wondered if the new job wasn't maturing him already.

"Last night Teresa Logan tried to kiss me in front of the Boxcar, and I overreacted."

"That's not what I believe. I think you reacted exactly the right amount," I said.

Stephen sighed a moment. "How exactly did you overreact?"

"I yelled at her and called her a few names that I'm not particularly proud of now, but I was upset."

"That she tried to kiss you?" the chief asked, his glance darting over to me for a moment to gauge my own reaction to the conversation. As a change of pace if nothing else, I was keeping my cool, at least for the moment.

"Let me guess. There were witnesses," the chief said slowly.

"At least three that I noticed immediately, but perhaps more," Jake admitted.

"So, that not only makes you look suspicious," he said as he looked at Jake, "but it makes you a suspect, too," the police chief said as he turned to me.

"I didn't have any reason to kill her! I just found out about what happened today."

"So of course, your first reaction was to storm down there and confront her about what happened," he said.

"Would you expect me to do anything less after hearing that particular bit of news?" I asked him pointedly.

"Take it easy, Suzanne. I'm not the enemy here. I'm just trying to establish a timeline as to what happened and when. After Jake told you what happened, I'm guessing that you weren't going there to congratulate Teresa on her taste in men," the police chief said.

"I was going to evict her, and then I was going to teach her a lesson about trying to steal someone else's husband, but I wasn't going there to kill her."

"Chief, I didn't tell her until half an hour ago," Jake said, "and that's the truth."

"I believe you both, but you know how folks around here are going to react. They're going to naturally assume that you went straight home and told Suzanne what happened last night. Why didn't you, by the way?"

Jake looked a little sheepish as he explained, "At first I thought it might all just blow over. After all, I spanked Teresa pretty hard when I rejected her. I figured she'd accept my rejection and leave me alone once and for all, so there was no reason dragging Suzanne into it."

"What made you change your mind today?" he asked, this time avoiding all eye contact with me.

Jake frowned for a moment before he spoke. "The truth of the matter is that I hated keeping it from my wife, no matter what the consequences that might arise by telling her."

"Why does everyone just assume that I'd go nuts over this?" I asked.

"Maybe because we know you," the police chief said, showing a slight grin for the first time since we'd seen him that day.

I wanted to be mad, but the truth was that I couldn't. After all, they were right. I had in fact marched over there to rip a wad of Teresa's hair out for making a move on my husband. I wouldn't have killed her, though. I stood by that belief, but I didn't feel any need to voice it at the moment. Goodness knew I'd probably have plenty of opportunities to do that later.

"You can see our position on this, Chief. That's why we have to dig into this. I hope we have your blessing," Jake said, letting his last word trail off into silence.

"And if I don't give it to you?" Stephen asked.

Jake just shrugged, not answering what everyone in the room knew anyway. If the chief refused to allow our investigation to occur, we'd just do it behind his back, and from the next thing he said, it was clear that he knew exactly that.

"You'll investigate Teresa Logan's murder anyway. Give me a second to wrap my head around this." Stephen leaned back in his chair and stared off into space for a full count of twenty before he spoke again. I knew the man had enough stress in his life at the moment to break the strongest person in the world, and unfortunately, Jake and I were adding to it, but we didn't have any more choice than he did. I just hoped he could see that. He'd been acting police chief for a while before Jake had stepped in, but the crown sat squarely on his brow now, and I had to wonder if the pressure of the job was already getting to him.

Finally, he sat forward and put his palms on his desk. "Okay, here's what we're going to do. You know I can't deputize you, don't you?" he asked Jake.

"I wasn't even going to ask you to," my husband said.

I wasn't following their line of logic. "Why not? I can't believe I didn't suggest it myself when you first walked into the room. Jake's a great cop, and you know it. Are you saying that you're beyond accepting help from a seasoned investigator?"

"My skill level is not the issue," Jake said patiently. "Look at it this way, Suzanne. I had his job not that long ago, and now, when his inaugural murder as permanent chief comes along, the first thing he does is make me his deputy. It screams that he doesn't have enough faith in himself to do the job without me, and if enough people believe that, he's sunk before he even has a chance to prove himself." He paused and glanced at Stephen. "Does that state the situation fairly?"

"I'd say so," the chief said. "It's nothing personal. If it were up to me, I'd put you on the case on the spot."

"Does that go for me, too?" I asked.

"Let's not cloud the issue," Stephen said, neatly dodging my inquiry. "Jake, you can't have any official status with this case, but we both know that I can't keep you from digging into it as a private citizen."

"I'm happy to hear that," Jake said with the hint of a victory smile.

"You didn't let me finish. That means that I can't allow you any special privileges, either. You can poke around, but you need to give my official investigation a wide berth while you do it."

"I'm not quite sure how to do that," my husband admitted.

"Lucky for you, you're married to an expert at it," he said with another grin. "I assume you two will be working together on this, am I correct?"

"I don't think we have much choice, do you?" I asked him.

"I can't admit to having an opinion about that one way or the other. All I'm saying is that you two both need to be careful. If there's any doubt in your minds about what you're doing, just ask me, and if you uncover anything that I don't know about, I expect an immediate report."

"That's kind of tricky, since we won't know everything you do unless you're willing to keep us informed, as well," I said. If we were lucky, the police chief would be reporting to us.

"We all know that's not happening. If you're in doubt, then over-communicate with me."

Oh, well. It had been worth a shot asking for inside information.

"If that's it, Chief, then we've got work to do," Jake said as he started to stand.

"Not quite. I need full statements from each of you. I can take them myself, or I can have one of my people do it," the chief offered.

"You've got enough on your plate without dealing with us, too," Jake said. "If you don't mind, I'll type them up, we'll sign them, and then I'll drop them back at your desk before we go. There's no sense in tying up your staff with us."

"Jake, you can't do that."

"Just watch me," he said with a smile. "I'm a wiz of a typist."

"Maybe so, but we're following standard procedure straight down the line on this case." Chief Grant grabbed his phone and punched in a few numbers. "Rick, I'm sending Jake Bishop and Suzanne Hart to your desk. Take their statements, type them up, and have them sign them before they leave."

As Jake stood, the new chief said, "I'm sorry about this, but my hands are tied."

"I understand completely," my husband said. "Thanks for the leeway you've given us with this."

"You're getting a little rope, but not much."

"Understood," he said, and then he turned to me. "Let's go, Suzanne."

"Bye," I said as I waved to Stephen. I'd known him since he'd been a lonely patrolman eating my donuts whenever he got the chance all the way to his rise to the top, and I wasn't about to let his new title intimidate me. After all, my stepfather had once held his job, as well as my husband. He might be the top man with the police force at the moment, and even my best friend's boyfriend, but he'd always be Stephen Grant to me.

After Jake and I told our brief stories to the officer in question, we signed our statements and left the station, but not before we had a dozen people stop and say good-bye to Jake as we were walking out the door.

"Now I know how it must feel to be married to a rock star," I said out on the sidewalk.

"Somehow I doubt that very much," he answered with a grin. "Are you hungry? I'm hungry."

"Is that some kind of secret code for asking me to go to the Boxcar Grill with you and interview people who might know what happened to Teresa?"

"No, it's a way of telling you that my stomach is growling, and it's time for lunch. We can work on the case after we eat, or even as we're waiting, but food is the first priority."

"Is that how you did it when you were with the state police?" I asked him as we walked through town toward the diner.

"Not usually, but then again, I never had a partner as pretty as you are. Why wouldn't I want to sit across the table and eat while I'm looking at you?"

"Don't expect me to answer that," I said with a smile. "I'm kind of surprised we got Stephen's blessing. Are you?"

"Not really, especially since he had to know that we were

going to look into this anyway. At least this way he's keeping himself in the loop of our investigation, which was pretty savvy on his part. When I was on the job, I'm not ashamed to admit that I took help from wherever I could get it, so I'm glad that he's not being stubborn about it. Our hands *are* sort of tied, though, and I'm not sure how we're going to get started."

"Watch and learn, my dear," I said as we neared the Boxcar Grill.

"You know what they say. When the student is ready, the teacher appears. Go on. Show me your stuff, Sweetie."

"Out here, in front of everybody?" I asked, pretending to be shocked by his suggestion.

"Not that stuff. At the moment, I'm more interested in your amateur sleuthing skills than your other considerable assets."

"I suppose I can do that, too, but it won't be nearly as exciting," I said as I winked at him.

"You can save that particular exhibition for later," he answered with a laugh. "Where do we start?"

We were just at the diner's steps. "The more I think about it, the more I realize that it might not be a bad idea if we table our discussion until after we've eaten after all. There are too many folks who will want to hear what we're going to be talking about in there."

"How can you possibly know that? We haven't even gone inside yet," Jake said.

"Trust me, I know the folks of April Springs. My investigations in the past have become some kind of fascination with a lot of them, so we really need to be careful about what we say in public."

"That's fine. You're the boss," Jake said. "We'll do whatever you say."

"I'm sorry, I didn't quite hear that. Would you mind repeating it?"

"What do you think?" he asked with a laugh.

"Hey, it was worth a shot," I answered as my husband and I went into the Boxcar together.

"Hello," Trish Granger said softly and dabbed at her eyes when we walked into the grill.

"Have you been crying, Trish?" I asked her as I took off my jacket, and Jake did the same.

She shook her head and tried to smile. "I've been helping out in the kitchen. I should know better than to chop onions. This always happens. It's all over town that you were the ones who found Teresa Logan's body. That's just awful."

"It wasn't pleasant," I said. I'd been afraid that she'd mention the attempted kiss the night before right outside her diner's door, but maybe she wasn't aware of it.

At least not yet.

"Take any seat that's free," she said as she handed us a pair of menus. She once more did her best to smile at us. "Sweet tea?"

"I was thinking about just having water today," I said.

"I can do that. What about you, Jake?" she asked, not responding to my unusual request.

"Actually, tea sounds good to me."

Trish nodded, and Jake and I found a table. We had barely sat when Trish showed up with two sweet teas.

"Where's my water?" I asked her as evenly as I could manage.

She frowned for a moment before she spoke. "I honestly thought you were kidding."

"I was," I said as I finally offered her a broad smile.

Trish didn't show much reaction, just offering a slight chuckle as she gave us our drinks. After she was gone, Jake asked me, "Suzanne, *were* you kidding with her earlier?"

"Of course I was. I may drink a ton of water everywhere else, but here, it's always going to be sweet tea, unless I get a soda as a change of pace, and Trish well knows that."

"You two are an odd pair of women; you know that, don't you?" Jake asked.

"That's probably why we're so close. Next to Grace, she's the best friend I've got in the world, not including you and Momma, of course," I said as I leaned over and patted his cheek.

"It's okay. I'm fine with that." Jake looked around suddenly and a dozen heads jerked away: back to their menus, their food, their hands, or even the floor. "You were right. Evidently, we're the stars of the show."

"Just wait until word gets out about what happened between you and Teresa last night," I said grimly. I didn't mind folks gossiping about us because we'd found the lawyer's body, but when they started pointing accusatory fingers at us behind our backs because of what had happened between her and Jake, then we were going to have a problem. I'd been the subject of police investigations in the past, as well as rampant idle speculation from the town's citizens about my guilt or innocence, and I didn't like either situation.

"We'll deal with it when it happens," Jake said as he reached over and patted my hand gently. It was a sweet gesture, and I was glad that I had someone like him in my life. Trish hadn't had any luck at all finding love with the exception of a man who'd been murdered soon after they'd started dating, and I couldn't help but hope that someday her Jake would find her, just as mine had found me.

After Trish came back and took our lunch orders, Momma walked in, searching the tables until she found us. A petite woman with more sass in her than a busload of teenage girls, my mother was frowning as she approached us, and I wondered what kind of trouble had visited her lately. Had she heard about

Jake's confrontation with Teresa, or was this possibly about something else?

"There you both are," she said as she took an empty chair. "I've been looking all over town for you."

"Did you hear about Teresa Logan?" I asked her.

"No, what about her?" Momma asked as she shed her coat.

"She's dead," I said simply, not knowing any other way of breaking the news to her.

"Oh, dear. That's terrible. She's awfully young to die. What happened to her? Was it a car accident? It wasn't suicide, was it? What a complete and utter waste that would be."

"I'm afraid someone killed her in her office," Jake said gravely. "Suzanne and I found the body not much more than an hour ago."

"That's horrible. What is this world coming to? Have they caught the killer yet?"

"No," I said simply. "If that wasn't why you were looking for us, what's up?"

"Suzanne, would you mind coming by the house this evening? Phillip and I need to speak with you."

"I have two questions for you. First, is Jake invited, too, and second, will there be food?" I asked her.

"You don't have to invite me, Dot. I won't be offended if this is family business."

"Hey, you're in this family, too," I reminded him. There was no way I was going to let my husband be excluded, no matter what was happening.

"The invitation was for both of you," she said. "Sorry I didn't make that clear. And yes, I'll be happy to feed you. Let's say six, shall we?"

"Momma, what's this about?" I asked her. We shared meals

at each other's homes occasionally, but usually nothing as formal as a personal invitation played a part in it.

"We'll discuss it this evening," Momma said as she stood.

"I brought you some sweet tea, Dot," Trish said from behind her.

"No thank you, dear, but Jake needs a refill. Let him have it," she said with a smile.

After Momma was gone and Jake had a second glass of sweet tea in front of him, he asked me, "What do you suppose that was all about?"

"I haven't the slightest clue," I admitted, "but I'm guessing that it's not good."

"Do you think she and Phillip are getting a divorce?" Jake asked me gravely.

"What? No! Of course not! He's wanted to be with her forever. He would never leave her."

"What if your mother were leaving him?" Jake asked.

"That can't be it. Jake, she's smitten with him. Great. Now that's all I'm going to be able to think about until tonight. Hang on. I'm going to find out what's going on right now."

Jake tried to grab my arm, but I sidestepped him. Trish was bringing our meals out as I slipped past her as well. "I'll be right back."

"Fine, but don't let this get cold," Trish said with a frown.

"I won't."

I hurried out into the parking lot, but I was too late.

Momma was already gone.

Apparently I'd have to wait until this evening to find out what was going on after all.

Fifteen minutes later, I pushed my nearly empty plate away. We'd both ordered the special, which had featured meatloaf, mashed potatoes, and green beans, along with a fresh dinner roll and a small pat of butter. I'd eaten more than I should have, but that was often the way I behaved when everything was so tasty, and I was upset about something. For some reason, my mother's invitation had left me anxious about the news that was too important to share in the diner. "I'm stuffed," I told my husband. "How about you?"

"Actually, I was thinking about having a piece of pie," Jake said with a slow smile.

"You do realize that Momma's going to have dessert tonight, don't you?"

"I know, but that's a good six hours from now," he protested.

I stopped him cold before he could go on. "I'm just doing what you told me to do. Since you quit working, you only get one dessert per day. You're the one who made me promise to keep you strong in case you wavered."

"I know, but I thought I'd make an exception today."

"That's fine with me. If you really want some pie, then you should get it," I said, refusing to be his dessert police officer. Ultimately he had to decide for himself what he ate. I had enough trouble watching my own caloric intake. I didn't need to watch his, too.

"I probably shouldn't," Jake said reluctantly.

"Either way, it's your decision," I answered with a shrug. I'd voiced the protest he'd made me promise to give him. After that, it was his decision.

As he paid our check, Trish asked, "What, no pie today?"

"Don't get him started," I said as I grinned at her.

"No pie it is," she said as she took his money and made change. "I'm sure that I'll see you both later."

"We'll be around," I said.

Before I could get out the door, Trish called out and asked me, "Suzanne, what's going on with your mother?"

"What do you mean?"

"When she left here, she acted as though the place were on fire," Trish said. "I can't ever remember her coming into the Boxcar and not eating."

"I don't know what's going on, but apparently I'm going to find out tonight," I replied.

"The world keeps getting stranger and stranger, doesn't it? I wish it made sense at least once in a while," Trish said as Jake and I headed outside.

We didn't get far, though, without being stopped by one of our neighbors.

Had it already started? Was this the beginning of the recriminations and accusations that were surely about to come our way?

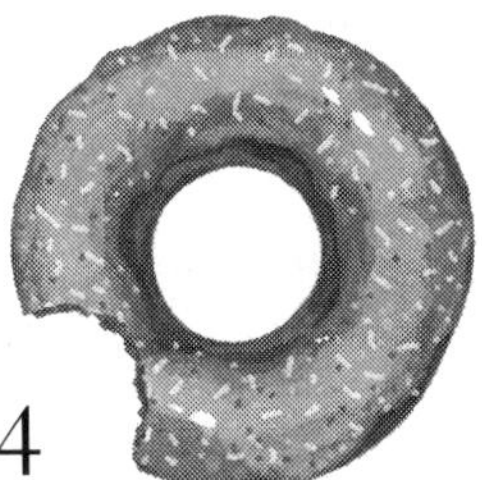

CHAPTER 4

"I THINK IT'S REALLY BRAVE OF the two of you to show your faces around town, given what's happened," Gabby Williams said to my husband and me.

"I hardly think it's brave of us to be seen in public, Gabby. It's not exactly our fault that Teresa was murdered. Finding the body was just bad luck on our part," I said.

"I'm not talking about that," she said, looking at us both askance for a moment. "I'm referring to Jake's knock-down-drag-out fight with the poor woman last night. Jake, do you know if you were the last person to see her alive?" Gabby asked him directly.

"No, I know of at least one other person who saw her after I did," Jake answered calmly.

"Who might that be?" Gabby asked earnestly, clearly intent on learning a new bit of gossip from my husband.

"It's pretty obvious, isn't it? We know for a fact that at least the killer saw her after I did," Jake replied. "Who knows how many other people saw her as well?"

"Of course," Gabby said, as though she clearly didn't believe one word of it.

"I'm curious about something," I said. "How did you hear about Jake's argument with Teresa?"

"Surely you're jesting, Suzanne. He wasn't exactly keeping his voice down, and my shop isn't that far away from the diner. My dear, I could hear him shouting from the front door of

ReNEWed." The store she named was her gently used elegant clothing shop, a bit of an oxymoron if you ask me, but Gabby did great business, and there was no doubt in my mind that her monthly profits far exceeded mine at the donut shop.

"It was just a simple disagreement," Jake explained. "It could have just as easily happened with someone else."

I thought that possibility was highly unlikely, but I wasn't about to mention it, since I didn't want to give Gabby anything else to dig her claws into.

"I doubt that very much," Gabby said, "though I do understand that you weren't the only man around town the young attorney fancied."

"Really? Like who, exactly?" I asked.

"Is that correct, or is 'whom' proper in that case?" Gabby asked me, clearly enjoying herself.

"I don't care one bit about the grammar one way or the other," I said. "I'm looking for information. Gabby, do you know something?"

"I know a great many things, such as when it is usually proper to use 'who' or 'whom,'" Gabby said, getting in another dig.

Enough was enough. "You know you're going to tell us eventually, so you might as well do it now," I said with a smile, trying my best to hide my frustration with the irascible woman.

When Gabby realized that I wasn't going to react to her goading, she frowned at me for a moment or two before she spoke again. "If I were you, I would speak with Robert Wells."

For a second I didn't know who she was talking about. Then I got it. "Bobby? Bobby Wells? The bag boy at the grocery store?"

"He's eighteen years old, Suzanne, and he prefers Robert," she informed me.

"I'll call him Little Miss Sunshine if it will help speed this along. Are you saying that Teresa's been flirting with him, too?"

"Suzanne, she flirted with *most* of the men in this town. You just chose not to notice until it hit a little too close to home for you." Gabby raised one eyebrow in my husband's direction, and I knew, though he'd kept quiet up until then, that was now about to be over.

I was right.

"Gabby, I did nothing to encourage Teresa Logan's attention, and when she tried to escalate things between us, I shut her down, and hard."

"Of course you did," Gabby said, nearly purring.

It was all I could do not to smile. Gabby Williams was messing with the wrong foe. I was pretty sure that she fully realized she could get away with something like that with me, but what she didn't understand was that Jake wasn't going to just roll over and take it. My husband took a step closer to her to remind her exactly who she was dealing with, and as he spoke, he made sure to hold eye contact the entire time. "You need to get this straight right here and now. If I'd been interested in that woman, no one would have heard a sound out of me. Is that what happened? No, it did not. I happen to be in love with my wife. She's everything to me, and anyone who thinks otherwise can go bark at the moon, as far as I'm concerned. Are we clear?"

"Crystal," Gabby said, and then, to my surprise, she smiled broadly at him. "You've got spunk, haven't you?"

I thought Jake was going to lose his temper, but then to my surprise, his angry response died in his throat and he began to laugh. "Sure. I've got that, all right, and a big dose of moxie, too."

"Suzanne, he's a keeper," Gabby said to me. "Don't you two worry about a thing. If I hear a word against either one of you, they'll rue the day they spoke it in front of me."

"We'd appreciate that," I said, doing my best to hide my bewilderment as to what exactly had just happened. Frankly, I was a little puzzled by it all. Had my husband just faced down the Beast of Springs Drive and actually won the confrontation?

Apparently he'd even done it well enough to gain a new ally. "Is there anything else you can share with us?"

"As a matter of fact, there is. Apparently Robert—oh, you're right about that; calling him Robert is ridiculous. He's always been Bobby to me. The most he's ever going to get is Bob, and he's going to have to earn that. Anyway, it appears that Bobby took the flirtation a little more seriously than it was intended. I happened to be near the produce section yesterday afternoon when he confessed his undying love for Teresa to her while she was getting a salad from the bar there. She clearly thought he was joking at first, but when she saw that he was serious, she scolded him as though he were a little boy. I thought Bobby was going to explode on the spot, and he nearly knocked me down as he raced for the back door."

"No wonder. He had to have been humiliated," Jake said.

"I didn't see any humiliation in him, only rage. To me, he looked as though he could have killed her on the spot." Gabby let that thought hang in the air for a moment or two before she added, "If I were you, I'd speak with him, and soon, before he runs away from April Springs and no one ever sees him again."

"Do you happen to know where he lives?" I asked her.

"It's hard to miss. He's staying in an old camper out behind St. Theresa's right now. The land has been in his family for a long time, but from what I've heard, the new rector is none too happy with his living arrangements."

"Thanks, Gabby," I said, and Jake offered her a smile. "We'll look into it."

She looked pleased with herself as she said, "You're most welcome."

Jake and I picked up my Jeep, which was still parked behind the donut shop, and as my husband and I headed for Bobby's place,

I asked him, "I've got to tell you, I'm really impressed. How did you manage that?"

"Manage what? I don't know what you're talking about."

"Come on, you know exactly what I'm referring to. You pulled that woman's fangs without the least bit of effort on your part," I said. "I thought Gabby was going to start purring there for a second."

"Suzanne, she was trying to bully us both, and the only way to deal with that kind of behavior is to walk right up and punch the bully in the nose."

"I thought you were actually going to do that for a second."

"I don't mean it literally. She just needed a reminder that she wasn't the top dog, and after I nipped a little at her, she fell right in line."

"Can you teach me how to do that?" I asked him. That could be the most useful skill I could ever master, given some of the folks I dealt with on occasion.

"Sorry. It's more of an inherent thing than one that can be taught," he said with a laugh as I pulled up beside Bobby's camper. No wonder the church wanted it to be relocated. It had to be at least forty years old, and it was a miracle that it had made the transition to its spot in the first place. At one point someone had clearly tried to spray-paint the old finish, but they hadn't done a proper job of prepping the material first, and large curly flakes were now pulling away everywhere. Both tires of the trailer were low to the point of being flat, and an old bucket served as a step up into the RV. Just beside the trailer was a small portable greenhouse, and when I glanced in through the plastic shell, I saw three rose bushes thriving inside, grouped around a portable space heater and looking quite toasty despite the cold. Instead of grass or gravel inside, the bed of the greenhouse was made up of red clay dirt. It appeared that the grocery clerk was a bit of an amateur horticulturalist in his off hours. Near the edge of the woods well away from the trailer and the greenhouse, there was a beat-up old storage shed with a door that barely closed.

"I don't see any cars around," Jake said as he looked around the property before we approached the front door.

"From what I've heard, he's got a car, but it doesn't run most of the time. Maybe it's in the shop again. All I know is that every time Bobby drives past the donut shop, he's on his motorcycle. I don't know why he doesn't just get rid of his car altogether."

"I doubt a motorcycle would be much fun in the snow, but if his car is in the shop now, maybe he's here after all. That shed looks big enough to hold a bike. Let's see if anyone's home." Jake ignored the bucket step and stayed on the ground as he banged on the front door. I could see the thin material buckling under the stress from his assault.

The camper door opened, and Bobby Wells peered out. He was wearing the same pattern flannel shirt and faded blue jeans that I always saw him around town in. He must have bought half a dozen identical shirts at the same time, and there was a bit of red clay dirt on his shoes. No doubt he'd been out working with his roses earlier, but was there more significance to the clay than that? "What's going on, Chief?" he asked the moment he saw my husband.

"I'm not the chief anymore," Jake said automatically, something I wished he'd keep to himself. I hadn't wanted him to lie to the young man, but if Bobby had been under the impression that Jake was still in charge of the police force, he might have been more receptive to our questions.

"Hey, Suzanne," he said as he noticed me for the first time. "What can I do for you both?"

"Where's your car, Bobby?" I asked him.

"I'm picking it up from the shop in twenty minutes. Why?"

"Just curious. I just didn't see it when we drove up."

"Is that why you're here?" he asked me incredulously. "What's wrong with my car? It passed inspection the last time, so I'm legally driving it, if that's what you want to know."

"We're not here about your transportation; we're here about Teresa Logan," I said, and Bobby immediately clouded up.

"What about her?"

"We heard you two had quite an altercation at the grocery store yesterday," Jake said. There was no question posed in his voice as he stated it matter-of-factly.

Bobby was clearly unhappy about this turn in the conversation. "I thought she wanted to date me. Apparently I was wrong. We didn't have a confrontation. It was more like a conversation."

"That's not the way we heard it," Jake replied, keeping his voice cold and narrow as he spoke. It was an effective interviewing technique, but I knew that I could never pull it off. I had the feeling that getting that "cop voice" down pat came only after being on the police force for awhile.

Bobby sneered a little before he spoke. "I'll just bet I know who's been talking about me. Surely you don't believe Gabby Williams. That woman would lie when the truth would suit her better."

I was glad that Jake didn't confirm or deny our source. Gabby had done us a favor by telling us about what had happened in the grocery store, and I didn't want to betray her confidence in return. "Son, there were quite a few people in that store. You shouldn't spread wild allegations."

Bobby shrugged. "You know what? It doesn't matter. I don't care who told you. Was I embarrassed by Teresa's rejection? You bet I was. She's been flirting with me ever since she got into town. How was I supposed to know that she didn't mean one bit of it? Is that really why you're here? Did she complain about me? That's just perfect. First I ask her out, just like I thought she wanted. Then she treats me like an idiot, and if that's not bad enough, the manager saw it all, and he fired me on the spot! Yesterday was a rotten day, and I hope I never see that attorney again as long as I live. You can tell her that for me the next time you see her."

Was it possible that he hadn't heard the news, or was he just acting as though he hadn't? His tone seemed sincere enough to me, but then again, I'd been fooled before by killers, and I'm sorry to say on more than one occasion.

"I'm afraid she's dead, Bobby," Jake said in that solemn way that refuted any denials before they could be formed.

He looked shocked to hear the news. "What? How? What happened to her?"

"Someone hit her in the back of the head with a bookend," I said.

"No. Seriously? That's terrible. She can't be dead. I mean, I just saw the woman yesterday."

"So you said," Jake replied calmly. If my husband was feeling any sympathy for the young man at all, he was a master of not showing it.

"Is *that* why you're here? Do you think I killed her? You're both insane. I didn't do it!" His voice was nearly a squeal as he denied his involvement in the attorney's death.

"Bobby, this is important. Did you happen to see her after your, ah, conversation at the grocery store?" I asked him.

"No, and that's the truth. I went to the back to cool off a little, and then I got fired almost immediately after that. What else could I do? I came straight back here and played video games until I fell asleep. It had to be three or four in the morning, and you just woke me up."

Jake turned and pointed toward the building I owned, which now happened to be a crime scene. I hadn't realized we could see it from where we stood, but my husband had. "Her office isn't that far away, is it? Teresa was working late last night; we know that much. What happened? Did you see the light on in her office and decide to go make her pay for humiliating you in public like that and getting you fired? It's perfectly understandable. Nobody could blame you for wanting to show her that she couldn't get away with treating you like that."

Wow, the way Jake had just laid it out, the entire thing was completely plausible. If I didn't know any better, I would have said that Jake had witnessed the murder himself, he was so convincing. No wonder so many guilty folks confessed their crimes after spending a little time with my husband.

"That's not what happened at all!" Bobby protested, and I could swear that he was on the brink of tears.

"Talk to us, Bobby. We can't help you if you don't come clean with us." Jake's voice was eerily soothing as he spoke.

Was Bobby about to break down and tell us something that we didn't already know? It turned out that we'd never find out, because the next thing I knew, Chief Grant was hitting his siren and pointing his squad car straight at us.

"Hi, Chief," Jake said, doing his best not to look displeased by Chief Grant's sudden arrival.

"What's going on here?" the chief asked.

"We were just having a friendly little chat with Bobby here," Jake said.

"Is that true?" the chief asked the teenager.

"I wouldn't call it friendly. They both think I killed Teresa Logan. Does that sound friendly to you?" Bobby asked, his voice on the edge of hysteria. "I didn't do it, and that's the honest truth!"

"How did you even know we were here?" I asked the police chief.

He pointed toward Teresa Logan's office, much as Jake had done earlier. "I was over there when I saw you two pull up. Is there a particular reason you're speaking with young Mr. Wells, if it's not to accuse him of murder?"

"He had a confrontation with Teresa Logan yesterday at the market," I explained. "In fact, he got fired because of her."

"What happened, Bobby?" the chief asked the young man.

"I asked her out, she turned me down, and my boss didn't like me asking at the store, so he canned me on the spot. I didn't kill her, though. I swear it!"

"Give me one second. Why don't you go inside and wait in there for me," Chief Grant said as he held up one finger, and then he turned to us. "May I have a word with the two of you?"

The chief had formed it as a question, but there was nothing optional about his request.

"What's going on, Jake?" he asked softly after Bobby was safely back inside.

"We heard that Bobby and Teresa had an argument at the grocery store yesterday, so we wanted to check it out," Jake admitted.

"I thought you were going to call me with any new information you got," Chief Grant reminded him.

"We were going to, but we didn't even know if there was any truth to the story or not. Naturally we wanted to confirm that it was worth your time to investigate before we called you," Jake said.

"You almost make it sound believable when you say it that way." The chief looked unhappy, and he waited three beats before he spoke again. "I was afraid this was going to happen. I'm almost used to getting it from Suzanne, but now you, too?"

"Hey, I resent that," I said.

"That's fine with me, but do you deny it?" the chief asked me.

I couldn't, so I kept my mouth shut, which was a genuine change of pace for me.

Chief Grant went on. "That's what I thought. Now I need to be able to trust the two of you, or this isn't going to work."

"I'm sorry," Jake said. "I can see now that I was wrong. I'll let you know everything we suspect from here on out."

"You don't have to go that far, but if you're going to talk to a potential suspect, I'd appreciate a heads-up. Is that too much to ask?"

"No, sir, it's not," Jake said, doing everything but saluting the man.

"Okay. I'm glad we got that settled. Now I think I'll have a go at him myself. I'll see you two later."

"That sounds good," Jake said.

We watched as Chief Grant knocked on the door before climbing up into the camper and then closing it behind him.

"Did you really mean what you just said?" I asked Jake as we walked back to my Jeep.

"I did," he said.

"You're honestly going to tell him every time we go speak with someone? He's never going to let us interview another witness. You know that, don't you?"

"Suzanne, there are some things we can skirt, others we can't. Don't worry about it."

"If you say so," I answered, still puzzled by how quickly my husband had caved in. "What do we do now if we can't speak with anyone without the chief's permission?"

"I say we drive back to the cottage and compare the pictures we took with our phones at the crime scene. That was one of the reasons I agreed to keep him informed about who we're going to speak with during our investigation. I was afraid he was going to confiscate our cell phones on the spot, and then where would we be?"

"That's brilliant," I said. "I didn't even consider that possibility. How did you come up with it?"

He grinned at me before he answered. "Maybe it's because that's exactly what *I* would have done. Now come on. Let's go before he figures it out for himself."

"Fine, but we probably shouldn't go home. In case the chief thinks of it, we don't want to be anywhere he can find us."

"Where should we go, if we don't go back to the cottage?" Jake asked.

"Let's park in front of the donut shop, and then we'll walk over to City Hall. He'll never think to look for us there."

"No, but I'm not sure there's any place we can hide from him in the building that he can't find us," Jake said.

"That one's easy. We use part of George's office."

"The mayor might not be willing to give us sanctuary, given the circumstances," Jake said.

"Not if he were here, but I happen to know for a fact that he's on his way to see an old friend. He stopped off at the donut shop this morning, and he told me he wouldn't be back until tonight."

"We can't just break into his office, though."

I couldn't believe it. *Now* my husband was deciding to be a law-abiding citizen, after keeping information from his former protégé that might be valuable in solving the homicide? "No worries on that point. We don't have to break in."

"Even if you have a key, I don't like using the mayor's office without his permission," Jake said.

"We're not exactly using his office, at least not technically, so we don't need his permission."

"I'm confused," Jake said.

I explained, "There's a small vestibule near his office that's tough to see from anywhere but sitting at the mayor's desk. We can compare our photos there without much danger of being discovered."

"Remind me never to play hide-and-seek with you," he said with a grin as we parked my Jeep in front of Donut Hearts.

As we walked down the street to City Hall, I grinned at him. "If you and I were playing hide-and-seek, there would be one big difference."

"What's that?" he asked.

"I'd be sure to let you find me."

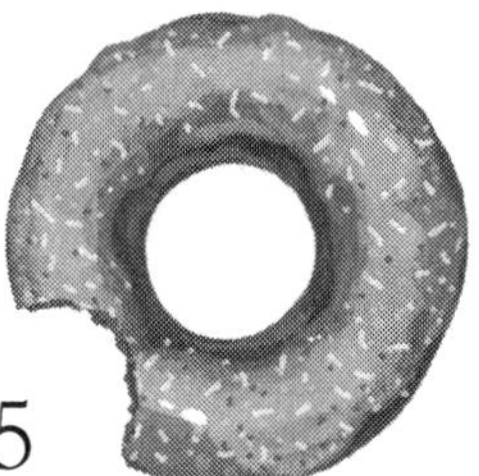

CHAPTER 5

"HOW DID I NEVER NOTICE this space before?" Jake asked me as I showed him the spot I'd chosen for us to work.

"It's easy to miss if you aren't standing in just the right spot," I told him. There was no door for the entry to the side room, but the way the walls had been built, from every angle but one, it appeared that there was no opening there at all.

"How did you find it?"

"I came by to see George one day, and he showed it to me," I said. There was just room enough for a pair of chairs and a small table. "I think he hides in here when he doesn't want anyone to know where he is. It's a lot easier to sneak over here when there's no one at the desk out front."

"Why doesn't the mayor have his own secretary?" Jake asked.

"George has his own explanation for it, but I think it's because he's just too irresistible to the women he hires."

"George? George Morris? Are you sure we're talking about the same man?" Jake asked me incredulously.

"Don't kid yourself. For women his age, he's a real catch. He's got an important job, he's polite, and he actually listens to you when you talk. I know he may seem gruff on the outside, but when you dig deep enough, he's a real sweetheart."

"How deep do you have to dig to find that side of him?" Jake asked me with a grin.

"You aren't a woman. You wouldn't understand."

"I can't tell you how glad I am about that fact."

Once we were seated inside the room, Jake and I pulled out our phones and started studying the pictures we'd taken. Jake had one of his small notebooks with him, the type he'd always carried when he'd been a cop, and the moment he found something interesting, he started jotting down things in it.

"Hey, did you just find something?" I asked him. "You're not a solo act anymore, mister. You need to share anything you come across with me."

"Sorry. You're right," he said. "I just wanted to write down the names of Teresa's two appointments last night. They both occurred after she and I had our little confrontation in front of the Boxcar Grill, so we know for a fact that she was alive up until then."

"Who exactly did she have meetings with?" I asked him. I could have looked it up on my phone just as easily, but Jake seemed to enjoy telling me himself, and who was I to disagree?

"Joe Chastain was scheduled to come in at seven thirty, and Becky Rusch had an appointment for eight thirty. It's kind of odd that Teresa conducted office hours that late in the day, isn't it?"

"I would think so," I said. "Then again, maybe it was the only time either one of them could meet with her. I know Becky, and Joe's been in the donut shop a time or two. I must admit, I'm not all that surprised they both needed an attorney."

"What makes you say that?" Jake asked me.

"According to local gossip, Joe is a mean drunk, and he likes to pick fights when he's intoxicated, so that's probably how he got into trouble. Becky's got a bit of a temper as well, but she doesn't have to be drunk to display it. I overheard a conversation a few months ago between two of my customers in the donut shop about her. Apparently, a man cut her off in traffic on the way to Union Square, and she got so mad that she chased him down and forced his car into a ditch. That's got to be why she hired Teresa."

"So, they both have anger issues, and the victim just happened to be killed with a bookend in what looks to be a crime of rage. Each one of their tempers makes sense, given what happened to Teresa," Jake said. He tapped his notebook before he added, "We need to speak with Becky first."

"Why do you say that?"

"If she admits to being there for her meeting, then chances are good that Joe is off the hook, since it would mean that Teresa had to have survived their appointment."

"Unless he came back and killed her after Becky left," I said.

"Maybe, but everything about this shouts that it was a spontaneous crime. As a general rule, you don't have an argument, leave and stew about it until later, and then return to pick up a nearby object and bash someone over the head with it."

I thought about that and then came up with an alternate solution. "That makes sense, but what if the killer just wanted us to *think* that it was spur of the moment instead of being a carefully planned execution?"

Jake laughed. "Suzanne, you've been reading too many mystery novels. You're giving the killer too much credit. Nine cases out of ten, a crime scene is exactly what it looks like."

"Maybe so, but didn't you handle all of the cases that weren't the norm when you were with the state police?"

"Mostly," Jake admitted. "I suppose we'll have to entertain the possibility that this was premeditated, but I'm not going to make it my main theory. I still think we need to talk to both of them, so we might as well start with Becky Rusch."

"That's fine with me, but let's finish this up first," I said. As I flipped through my shots, I noticed something odd in one of them.

Jake must have seen the puzzled expression on my face. "What is it, Suzanne? Did you find something?"

"I'm not sure."

"Let me see," he said as he scooted closer and tried his best to look over my shoulder.

I held the phone toward Jake and showed him the picture in question.

"It looks like some kind of packing label to me. What do you think?" I asked.

"Where exactly did you take this photo?" Jake asked as he kept studying the image.

"It was back behind the desk," I answered. "See the chair leg at the edge of the shot? It's the one closest to Teresa and away from the client chairs on the other side. I can tell because it's the leg that's been scratched up. I noticed it when we moved it in, because Teresa tried them all out and then claimed that it was more comfortable than the other chairs." The office had been leased fully furnished, so Momma had graciously donated some office furniture she had in storage from other projects of hers. I'd taken it all gratefully, since I really couldn't afford to outfit the place with new stuff before I even collected my first month's rent.

"I agree; it's some kind of label. My question is, what did it come from, and how did it end up in Teresa Logan's office?" he asked me.

I enlarged the picture as much as my phone would allow, but all I could see was part of a bar code. "I have no idea."

"Then we'll just have to file it away and keep looking. No doubt the chief found it as well. He might even know where it came from," Jake said.

"Only we don't have any way of finding that out," I answered.

"We just have to do the best we can with what we've got. Hey, here's something interesting," he added almost instantly.

I leaned over to see what he'd captured on his phone. It was nothing more than a smudge of something on the carpet, and I had a tough time seeing what it was. After a few moments, I had a guess, though. "Is that clay dust?" I asked him.

"That's what it looked like to me when I took the picture," Jake said as he frowned. "I could swear at the time that the imprint showed the back edge of a shoe or boot. I'd been hoping my phone would pick it up, but clearly it didn't. All I can see here is a smudge of something that may or may not be red clay."

"I'm sure the chief must have seen it, too," I said. "They probably got a great picture of it."

"Yes, but that doesn't do us much good, does it?" It was clear my husband was getting frustrated with the limitations an investigation on the other side of the law imposed.

"What about that message on Teresa's machine?" I asked as we finished going through our photos without finding anything else that looked significant to us. At least we'd gotten a few things out of them. After all, our images of the appointment book had given us two solid suspects that we wouldn't have had if I hadn't flipped that appointment book open.

The problem was, Chief Grant knew about them as well.

"Why don't you play that message again?" he suggested.

I did, twice as a matter of fact. After it ended the second time, I said, "Beats me. There's something familiar about it, but I can't put my finger on it."

"At least you're doing better than I am, because I don't recognize the voice at all," Jake admitted. "If he'd been speaking in a calm voice, it might have been easier to tell who it was, but he seemed pretty upset, didn't he?"

"I'm not really all that surprised. I would think that Teresa got those kind of calls on a regular basis," I said.

"What makes you say that?"

"She was a lawyer, Jake. Given the quality of her general clientele, I'm guessing that civility was usually at a minimum."

"I'm not so sure you're being a hundred percent fair about that. Don't forget, innocent people need attorneys sometimes, too."

"You're right. It just seemed to me that Teresa wasn't that kind of lawyer. Then again, maybe my attitude toward her has been tainted by her behavior toward you since she first came to town."

"I'm not saying she was right to do what she did, but you can't condemn her for the class of her clients. Let's get back to that message. It's one thing being angry with your opponent's attorney, but it's a whole new level to actually kill her just because of a lawsuit."

"It's still a possibility, though. Until we figure out who left that message, we've got two names and three clues," I said as I closed up my phone. "That's not bad, considering that we've just gotten started."

"It's not exactly good, either."

"Don't you think you're being a little too hard on us?" I asked my husband.

"Maybe. You have to remember that when I was a cop, I had access to everything pertinent to the case the moment it was discovered. We're in the dark about a great deal involving this case. I admit it; I'm frustrated."

"Welcome to my world," I said as I gently touched his shoulder. "I know that we're on the outside looking in, but that gives us an advantage, as well."

"What's that?" he asked, clearly not believing me for an instant.

"We don't have to follow the same rules that you did when you were a part of law enforcement," I answered with a grin.

"I'm not breaking into someone's house, if that's what you're suggesting," Jake said with a frown.

"I wasn't, but I would even go that far if I thought it was important enough," I told him. "We need this case solved just as much as the April Springs police department does. The worst thing that could happen to us would be if the killer were never caught. Besides, we're not just doing this for our sakes; there's also the need for justice to be served, not to mention honoring Teresa Logan's memory. I might not have been the woman's biggest fan, but she deserved better than she got."

"So, do you have any suggestions as to what we should do after we speak with Joe and Becky?" Jake asked me. He clearly was at a loss on how to operate from this side of the law, and I felt a little sorry for him.

"Absolutely. We need to dig into Teresa's life a little deeper than we have so far. She's made quite an impression on the people of April Springs during her short time here. Somebody in town knows something about her personal life. I guarantee it."

"I don't doubt it, but how do we find out who to even speak with?"

"It's not going to be easy. We just start asking questions and see what kinds of answers we get."

"But that's going to wait until we speak with Teresa's last two appointments, right?" Jake asked.

"By all means. Let's go have a chat with Joe and Becky." Jake frowned at me for a moment. "What's wrong?" I asked him.

"I don't like the way this whole thing feels. We promised Stephen that we wouldn't go behind his back anymore, and we still haven't asked him for his permission to conduct those particular interviews."

"I'm not suggesting that we do," I said. "Jake, is there any doubt in your mind that he has already spoken with both of them by now?"

"There's not a chance that hasn't already happened. It's what any good cop would do, and despite the fact that he's a little young, Stephen Grant is a good cop."

"Then if he's had his first interview with each of them, he might not mind if we took our turn."

"Suzanne, do you think there's one chance in a hundred that he'd actually approve of that?"

"There's only one way to find out," I said as I stood. "Let's go ask him. This is a little too delicate to handle over the phone."

"That sounds good to me, but there's something else we need to do first."

"What's that?" I asked.

"We have to send our photos from our cell phones to the computer at home. That way, if the chief does decide to take them from us and make us delete our copies, we'll have backups there."

"Do you really think he might do that?"

"Suzanne, I'm just trying to plan for the unexpected. If we make the backups and he doesn't say anything about the photos, then we haven't lost anything. If he decides to make it an issue though, we'll be covered."

"Then let's do it. You're going to have to show me how to do it, though."

After a few trial-and-error moments, we had our photographic records backed up on our home computer. Jake was right. It was a good contingency plan. I still hoped that we wouldn't have to use it, though. If Chief Grant made us delete the images we'd taken of the crime scene, it most likely meant that he'd lost trust in us and our ability to work on this case together.

Chief Grant was at his desk, leaning back in his chair and frowning into space. Jake knocked on his door after getting permission to pass through upon signing us both in on the ledger.

"Is this a bad time?" my husband asked the police chief.

"Yes. No. I guess what I mean is that it's as good a time as any. Come on in," he said.

"That's not what I'd call a definitive answer," I said as we stayed outside.

"You're both more than welcome to come in. I was just mulling over the two interviews I just conducted, trying to figure out how I could have handled them better. To say that they were unproductive would be an understatement."

"Who did you interview?" Jake asked before I could admit that we wanted a shot at his two reticent subjects. Jake knew full well who the police chief had spoken to, but by asking a simple question, he'd still managed to tell a lie. It was an interesting thing to see in action.

"As if you didn't already know. You both saw the appointment book, didn't you? Of course you did," Chief Grant said, and then he shook his head slightly. "Why wouldn't you? The appointment book was open, and it was kind of hard to miss."

"We saw that Joe Chastain and Becky Rusch both had appointments with Teresa last night," I acknowledged, without telling him that I had been the one who had opened it to the one page we needed to see. It was an interesting way to hold a conversation, finding new ways to obfuscate the truth. I was a little sad that we were deceiving our friend, but I couldn't bring myself to come right out and admit that I'd been the one who'd opened the book in the first place.

"And now I'm betting that you two want to talk to them yourselves, is that it?" He was dead on the money, but he didn't look too happy about it.

"Would you mind if we gave it a try?" Jake asked. "We can approach them from a different angle than you were able to. What do you have to lose?"

"Just my job, my dignity, and my hope of ever being gainfully employed in law enforcement ever again," Chief Grant said. "Why not? You can't do any worse than I did."

"Don't be so hard on yourself," I said. "It's an extremely difficult job."

"I realize that more and more every day. I just hate it when folks won't cooperate when I ask them simple questions that should be easy to answer," he said with a grin.

"I can relate to that," Jake said.

"Somehow I kind of doubt that," the police chief said with a wry smile. "I'd be surprised if you didn't always get what you were looking for the first time out."

"Take my word for it; I've been just as frustrated by the lack of cooperation as you are right now. If you're sure you don't mind, Suzanne and I would love to interview both of them."

"Do you need any information from me about either one of them?" Stephen asked as he leaned forward to check his report.

"We've got it covered," I said quickly, not quite again lying but not telling the complete truth, either.

"You were taking pictures when I showed up at the office," the chief said. "No doubt you took a few photos of the page in question." There was no question, just a statement of fact.

"We did, along with some other things," Jake readily admitted. I didn't like where this was going, but we had to play it out as honestly as we could at this point. I didn't mind skirting the truth if I had to, but I wasn't going to lie directly to the police chief, particularly not about anything directly involving an active murder case, and I knew that Jake wasn't about to do it, either.

"What did you get?" the new chief asked hesitantly. "Was there anything of interest that you'd care to share with me?"

Jake grinned. "I didn't want to volunteer anything, but I was really hoping you'd ask." He pulled out his phone and brought up the pictures he'd taken at the crime scene. Skipping through them, he landed on the one we'd both studied so carefully earlier and said, "I tried to get a good shot of that heel print, but my camera couldn't pick it up."

"We got something better than that, but it was ruined when we tried to preserve it."

"Can you at least tell if a man or a woman made it?" I asked.

The chief shrugged. "All we can say for sure was that it was from some kind of work boot. We can't even gauge the size, but we're going on the assumption that it was made by a man."

"Women wear work boots, too, you know," I said.

"Of course they do. We're not going to discount that possibility, either, but I think that we can all agree that the majority of people who wear them are men. What else have you got?"

"Show him the picture you took that's been baffling us," Jake urged me, so I grabbed my phone and I pulled up the label I'd found by the desk.

"Chief, do you have any idea what that is?"

"It's from a box of power bars," he said with a nod. "We found that, too. Evidently Teresa bought a case of the things yesterday, and the label came off. We found the rest of the label, along with the box, in the office closet."

We hadn't even had time to search there! So that explained that. Or did it? "Do you happen to know if she ordered them online, or did she buy them at the grocery store?" I asked.

Chief Grant looked surprised by the question. "I have no idea. Why does it matter?"

Jake got it right away. "If they were from the grocery store, then Bobby Wells could have brought them to her, which would put him in her office sometime around the murder."

"I'll look into it," he said as he jotted down a quick note. "Thanks."

"We're more than happy to help. How's your investigation

going?" It was an innocent enough question, but I held my breath waiting for his response. I figured he could yell at us, ignore us, or there was even a slight chance that he'd tell us something we didn't already know. Thankfully Jake stayed out of it.

Stephen smiled. "I'm not quite sure that I'm ready to share that much with you two at the moment."

At least it was better than a scolding. "I get that, but if you change your mind, you know where to find us," I said.

Jake stood and offered the chief his hand. "Thanks for the green light on our interviews."

"At this point, what can it hurt, right?" he asked as he took it.

"I'm sure we'll see you soon," I said with a grin.

"There's no doubt in my mind."

"Suzanne, you pushed him a little in there, didn't you?" Jake asked me the second we were back in my Jeep. I didn't have to ask him what he was referring to.

"I figured, what could it hurt? The chief seemed to be in a giving mood. After all, he's letting us talk to Joe Chastain and Becky Rusch."

"I know, but it had to cost him something to allow it. Did you ever consider stopping while we were ahead?" my husband asked me with a laugh.

"It never even crossed my mind," I said with a big grin. "Do you still want to tackle Becky first?"

Instead of answering my question directly, my husband said, "Normally, I've always believed in handling the toughest interview first."

"So then we speak with Joe?" I asked.

"Funny, but I don't think he's the hardest one we have to talk to. I understand men like him, but Becky Rusch's road rage is something I'm having trouble wrapping my head around."

"Then it's Becky after all," I said, starting off in the direction of her place.

"No, it's Joe," he corrected me.

I turned around the moment I got the chance. "Make up your mind, sir."

"I never got a chance to tell you what my thoughts were," he countered. "We do this in order, and since Joe's appointment was first, he's the logical one to start with."

"Oh, if you're going to start trotting out logic, then I don't stand a chance." I knew that Joe Chastain worked at a body shop on the edge of town, so that was the way I started driving. "How are we going to handle this? Are we going to pretend that my Jeep needs a facelift?" I asked.

Jake looked surprised to hear the idea. "No, I thought we'd just come right out and ask him about his meeting with his attorney last night."

"We can try, but it might not work. We can't force anyone to talk to us, remember?"

"Maybe not, but I have a feeling that he's going to want to cooperate."

"Why do you think that?" I asked as we neared our first suspect's place of employment.

"I don't know. Folks just seem to want to open up to me," Jake answered.

He wasn't kidding. "Did you ever think that it might be because you carried a gun?"

"I'm sure that had a little to do with it, but I never had to use it to get a statement out of someone."

"Be my guest, then. I'd love to see you in action."

Jake wasn't sure what to make of my statement, and maybe he was right, but I had a hunch that without any authority backing him up, he might have just as hard a time getting answers as Grace and I usually did.

One thing was certain: we were about to find out.

CHAPTER 6

AT LEAST THE BODY SHOP wasn't busy.

I spotted Joe over to one side and told Jake, "He's over there eating a bag of chips." The repairman had on a pair of dirty overalls and heavy work boots that left a track of red clay dirt wherever he stepped. Had he left a similar trail the night before in the attorney's office? Even if he had, it didn't necessarily mean that he'd killed her, but if he tried to deny that he'd even been there, it might be something we could use against him later.

Jake nodded and started off. As he headed for the man, I followed along. There was no way I was going to miss this.

"You're Joe Chastain, aren't you?" Jake asked in an officious voice.

"Who wants to know?" Joe replied, clearly unimpressed so far.

"We need to ask you a few questions about Teresa Logan," Jake said rather formally.

"You a cop? You look like a cop to me," Joe said with a scowl.

"I used to be," Jake admitted.

"But you're not anymore," Joe replied. "I hate cops." Chastain wadded up his bag and threw it toward a nearby trashcan, hitting the floor instead. I had to fight the urge to pick it up and throw it away properly for him.

"Like I said, I'm not one anymore."

"Then I've got nothing to say to you. I already spoke to the police chief, but I didn't have much choice, did I?"

"He gave us his permission to follow up with you," Jake said. I could tell that he was beginning to get a little frustrated by the man's lack of cooperation. I wanted to step in to see if I could expedite the interview, but this was something Jake needed to see for himself. Besides, I doubted that Joe would have been any more cooperative with me than he was being with my husband, though I didn't have the weight of being a former police officer against me.

"Good for him," the man said. "The problem is that I don't have time to monkey around with you two." He glanced at me and added, "Shouldn't you be somewhere making donuts?"

"The shop's closed at the moment," I said with a smile. I regretted giving Emma our last donuts earlier. Maybe I would have been able to use them to bribe Joe into answering a few of our questions. It had worked with others in the past.

"Well, mine isn't," Joe said with contempt. "I'm busy, and even if I wasn't, customers aren't allowed back here."

"That works out fine, because we're not customers," Jake said, standing his ground.

The body shop repairman didn't like that one little bit. "Listen, I've already told you once, so I'm not going to say it again. I've got nothing to say to you."

He clearly didn't know that my husband's stubborn streak was wider than anyone else's he'd ever met. "Then we'll be glad to wait right here until you do," Jake replied.

Joe approached my husband, cracking his knuckles as though he were about to use them. I wanted to tell Jake that maybe it was time to back off, but I couldn't do it without embarrassing him, and besides, I knew that my husband could handle himself. He didn't need a gun to protect himself, or me either, for that matter.

"I said go." The repairman spat out his words, and the two men were inches apart now.

"No."

After the longest ten seconds I could recall in recent memory, Chastain backed off a few steps. "What do you want to know?"

"Did you meet with Teresa Logan last night at seven thirty in her office?" Jake asked as though nothing had just happened.

Joe frowned. "I don't have to tell you that. It's, what do you call it? Attorney–client privilege. Yeah, that's it."

Why was I not surprised that Joe Chastain knew his rights?

"I'm not asking what you discussed. All I want to know is if you met with her," Jake said patiently.

"Yeah, of course I did. So what?"

"Was anyone else around the office when you left?"

"No. The place was empty," Joe said.

"Was she on the phone with anyone as you were leaving, by any chance?" I asked.

Joe looked a little surprised to find me still standing there behind my husband. "Yeah, as a matter of fact, she was making a call right when I walked out the door."

"Did you leave a threatening message on Teresa Logan's answering machine within the past week?" Jake asked him.

Joe frowned and shook his head. "Why would I do that? She was my attorney, and besides, she was going to get me off. Now I'm going to have to start all over and go through the hassle of finding a new lawyer."

"I'm so sorry for the inconvenience," I said sarcastically. Here a woman was dead, and this man was worried about letting his fingers take a walk through the yellow pages. I had a tough time generating any sympathy for him. "Did you happen to catch who she was calling?"

"How would I know?" he asked.

"Joe, is there a problem over there?" a gruff, heavyset man asked the repairman from the office.

"No, it's all good, Mr. K."

The man nodded, and then he stared at us for a few moments before turning away.

"Listen, I can't afford to get fired," Joe said. "I need this job. I answered your questions. You have to take off now."

"Are you okay with that, Suzanne?"

"I don't have anything else for him at the moment," I said.

"Okay, then," Jake said. "We can leave. If you think of anything else, be sure to let us know."

"How about if I call the chief instead?" Joe asked with a nasty grin. "After all, he's the one working the job. You're not, remember?"

Back at the Jeep, I turned to my husband and smiled. "I must say that I'm impressed."

"Why? I didn't get very much out of him."

"The fact that he told us anything at all is what's so amazing to me. I thought he was going to take a swing at you for a second there."

"He was posturing, and when I wouldn't back down, he folded. If he'd been drunk, it might have been a completely different story, but I knew where things stood."

"I'm going to have to take your word for it, but I'm warning you, if you try to go toe to toe with Becky Rusch, things might not end nearly as well for you."

Jake seemed amused by the idea. "Why, do you think she might take a swing at me?"

"I don't know, but you said it yourself. She's a bit of a wild card. If you go over there trying to intimidate her, you're probably going to run into the same dead end that Stephen did."

"Do you want to show me how it's done? Is that what you're saying?" he asked with a grin.

"I'd love to take the lead, but feel free to jump in during a lull."

"Only if I have to," Jake said, and then he took out his cell phone.

"Who are you calling?"

"I'm going to update the police chief about our conversation, and then I'm going to ask him to check Teresa's cell phone records. If she really did make a call after Joe left, he might be off the hook."

"If he was telling us the truth," I said.

After Jake made his phone call, he asked me, "Don't you believe Joe's story, Suzanne?"

"The truth of the matter is that I've made it a point lately not to take anything a suspect tells me at face value," I said.

"It sounds as though you've been burned in the past."

"More times than I care to admit," I said.

"Where exactly does Becky Rusch work?" Jake asked me as I took a side street near the donut shop.

"She's a clerk at the flower shop," I said.

"It's hard for me to believe that someone who works for a florist ever committed road rage."

"Why shouldn't she? I run a donut shop, and there are days when my customers drive me so crazy I'd be tempted to run a few of them over if I were given the chance." I was speaking in hyperbole, and my husband knew it.

"It's a good thing you've got such a short commute from work to home, then," he answered with a chuckle.

We had to wait in line, since the flower shop was busy. I watched as Becky handled customer after customer with more patience than I showed at times at Donut Hearts. Becky Rusch was a rather plain woman, but she made up for it by smiling brightly at every customer, making each one of them feel as though their order was the most special one she'd take that day. When it was our turn at the front counter, Becky turned her charm on us as she said, "Hey, Suzanne. You must be Jake. What can I get you today?"

I glanced at the flower arrangements in the display case and said, "We'd like to buy something nice. How are the roses this time of year?"

"Sorry, but we're completely out. No worries, they're on back order, but we haven't had any since Valentine's Day. Our supplier has been having trouble meeting demand, but we should be getting some in next week."

"Suzanne, why exactly are we buying flowers?" Jake asked me.

"I thought it might be nice to take some to Momma's for dinner this evening."

"If you ask me, you can't go wrong with one of our party arrangements," Becky said. "I know some folks bring wine, but who doesn't like a burst of color in their lives?"

"Then again, you have to say that, since you're a florist," I said with a grin. It was hard to believe that this mild-mannered woman had committed an act of road rage.

"I've got a hunch that you recommend they bring donuts to the party. Am I right?" she asked me.

"Always," I said. "What's the freshest arrangement you have right now?"

"*All* of our flowers are fresh," Becky said loudly, and then, in a softer voice, she added, "I'd go with the spring bouquet if I were you. They just came in this morning."

"We'll take one," I said.

As I was starting to pay, I asked her, "It's a shame about what happened to Teresa Logan, isn't it?"

"It is," she agreed.

"Did you happen to know her?" I asked.

"I did," Becky said as she gave me my change.

"Was it privately or professionally?" Jake asked her. I had been under the impression that he'd be letting me handle this interview, but since I had interrupted his, it was only fair that he chimed in on mine occasionally.

Becky frowned a little before answering. "That's funny. I know you're asking a question, but you sound as though you already know the answer," she replied, her smile quickly disappearing.

"You were one of her law practice's clients," Jake said, again making it a statement instead of a query.

"I am, or I suppose the proper way to say it is that I was. Why did I need an attorney? I'm sure you already know the answer to that, too. I was having a horrible day, and I let my emotions get the better of me. I'm still paying for it, but it just won't go away."

"Did you meet with Teresa Logan last night?" Jake asked her.

"No, I did not," Becky said as she handed me the arrangement. There was no one left in the store, so she couldn't brush us off in order to wait on another customer, but I knew that she was going to find some excuse to get rid of us, so I had to act quickly.

"That's a little odd. Your name was in her appointment book," I said.

"I went to her office, but she never showed up. The truth is that I got tired of knocking on the front door, so I finally left. The next thing I know, the police chief comes over here this afternoon asking me about my relationship with her. What business is that of his, or yours either, for that matter?" The sunny side of her personality was definitely gone now.

"We're just trying to help," I said.

"Are you saying that you're trying to help *me*? Forgive me for saying so, but I sincerely doubt that."

"If you didn't kill your attorney, then why wouldn't you want her murder solved?" Jake asked, and I could tell that he was honestly curious.

"People get murdered every day all over the country. I'm sorry it happened, but I can't get too wrapped up in it," Becky said. "Besides, I was going to have to find a new attorney anyway. She wasn't doing me much good, and when she missed that appointment last night, I was going to fire her anyway."

Teresa had the perfect excuse for not making it, since there was a good chance that she'd been dead, but I didn't feel that was the right time to bring it up. I was about to ask her another question when my husband asked it for me.

"So, you're claiming that you never went inside her office the day of the murder?" Jake asked.

"That's not what I'm claiming; it happens to be the truth. Now if you'll excuse me, it's time to lock up for the day."

I glanced at the hours displayed in the front window and saw that she had another ten minutes left on her shift. "Is your boss in back going to get upset if you close up before it's time? Don't pretend that you're here alone. You made it a point earlier to tell us loudly that all of the flowers you have are fresh, though you recommended something that just arrived after that in a softer voice."

"It's not my boss; it's her daughter, and believe me, she'll jump at the chance to take off early. Do you honestly think she's going to tell her mother that I let her go before we were scheduled to close for the day? If you do, then you don't know Cindy at all. Now if you'll excuse me, I need to lock up and balance the cash register receipts."

There was no way I could think of to stall her, so I did the only thing I could think of doing. "Thanks for the flowers," I said lamely as I grabbed the arrangement, and then Jake and I made our way out the front door.

"Always happy to help," Becky said, and then the locks clicked into place as she bolted the door behind us.

"Okay, before you say anything, I know I pressed her a little too hard back there. I'm sorry," Jake said. "You just seemed to be taking forever to get to the point."

I shoved the flowers into his hands so I could drive. "That's usually what you have to do to get someone to cooperate with you that doesn't have to. You have to sneak around from the side instead of hitting them dead on in the face. It takes quite a bit of subtlety, Jake."

"Hey, I can be subtle if I have to be," my husband protested.

"Really? During an investigation?"

"I'm not saying that I've ever done it; I'm just saying that I could if I had to."

"Then start practicing, because you're going to need a whole new set of skills if you're going to make it on this side of the law."

"You make us sound like a pair of desperate bandits," he said with a frown.

"We're not criminals, but we're not in law enforcement, either. We're simply interested law-abiding citizens."

"Who happen to be nosey and intrusive," Jake added.

"Now you've got it."

"I really am sorry, Suzanne. I'll do better from now on."

"Don't worry about it. Becky clearly wasn't in the mood to say anything, anyway. We'll figure out another angle and work her from that."

"And in the meantime?" Jake asked me.

I glanced at my watch before I answered. "We're due at Momma's pretty soon. Maybe we should leave our investigation until later."

"That's fine with me. What do you suppose this is all about?"

"I wish I knew," I said. "I guess we'll find out soon enough."

Momma greeted us alone at the front door of her home. "Flowers! How lovely. Thank you both." After she hugged us both, she said, "You're early."

"What can I say? I couldn't wait," I said. I looked around and couldn't see her husband anywhere. "Where's Phillip?"

"Unless I miss my guess, he should be arriving at the Outer Banks soon," my mother said as she glanced at the clock on the wall.

"Did he go without you? What's going on? Are you two having trouble, Momma?"

"No, we're perfectly fine," she said. "The truth of the matter is that I urged him to go. I have some business I need to take care of here in town, and he's only going to be gone for a few days. After that, I'm joining him."

"That sounds nice. You work way too hard, so you deserve a vacation," I told her as Jake and I took off our coats.

"It's not just a vacation, Suzanne," Momma said. "Phillip and I are leaving April Springs as soon as we find a place on the coast."

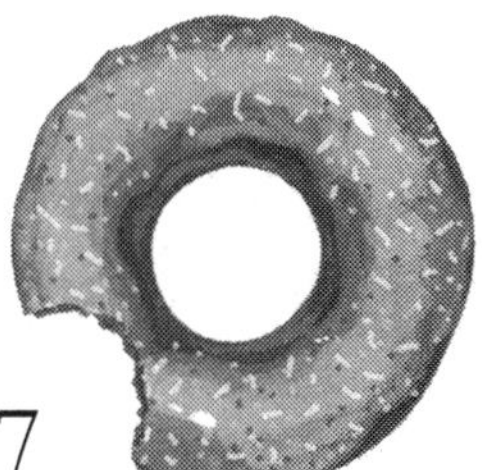

CHAPTER 7

"WHAT! WHAT DO YOU MEAN, you're leaving?" My mother had lived in April Springs her entire life, and I couldn't imagine her being anywhere else. If she and Phillip moved to the Outer Banks of North Carolina, she might as well move all the way across the country. Though the chain of islands was still in the state that we lived in, it was a good eight – to nine-hour drive, and I knew that I'd rarely see her if she made the move.

"Take a breath, child. Your face is turning red," Momma said.

"We're both having a little trouble understanding it, I guess. Why the move, Dot?" Jake asked her. His brow was furrowed as well, and I knew that he was extremely sympathetic to my distress. And why shouldn't he be? He'd have to listen to untold hours of complaining from me if this actually happened.

"It's simple, really. We need a fresh start," my mother told him, and then she turned to look at me. I was causing her distress with my reaction, something I hated, but I couldn't help it. I was in real pain just thinking about it.

"Are you the one who needs to move, or is it your husband?" I asked her point blank.

"We both do," Momma said firmly. There was a hint of warning in her voice as she said it, and I knew better than to criticize her husband.

"Who brought it up first, though?" I asked, pushing her

on it nonetheless. If this was going to happen, I needed to understand why.

Momma sighed deeply before she explained, "Since Phillip retired, he's been restless. I thought he'd found a suitable hobby digging into the past around here, but it doesn't seem to be enough anymore. Don't you worry, Suzanne. This will be good for us."

"Maybe for the two of you, but I'm telling you right now, if you go through with this, you're going to make me miserable," I said sullenly. I knew that I wasn't handling the news like a mature woman should, but this was my mother. I depended on her presence in my life every day. Thinking of being in April Springs without her was something I couldn't bear. All along I'd been under the impression that she'd needed to be close to me, but now that I was faced with the prospect of her absence, it seemed that I was the one who wasn't able to handle it.

"Stop treating this as though it's one of life's great tragedies! You can visit us whenever you'd like," Momma said, doing her best to reassure me.

"Really? Do you honestly believe that? Even if I take off the two days I get every week and come see you, it's going to seem like two days spent driving in the car. I can just see it now. I spend the first day driving, I get to see you for a few hours, go to sleep, and then drive back here."

"I'm sorry if it's going to be inconvenient for you, but it needs to be done," Momma said. It appeared that she was fighting to keep her own emotions in check. That was more than I was managing.

"Aren't you even going to miss me?" I asked, the tears coming unbidden.

"Of course I'm going to miss you," she said, her tears coming as she wrapped her arms around me. I wasn't sure how Jake was reacting to all of this at the moment, nor did I care. He was giving us space to work this out, which was the smartest thing he could do.

"Then don't go," I pled with her. Though my mother was quite a bit shorter than I was, I still felt like a little kid when she had her arms around me.

"We all must do things for our marriage that we might not do otherwise," Momma said as she started to pull away and dabbed at her tears. "Now, let's eat. I made us all a lovely pot roast for dinner."

"I'm sorry, but I've suddenly lost my appetite."

"Suzanne, it would be rude to just leave," Jake said.

"It's fine. Let her go," Momma said. Before I could bolt out of there, she took my hands in hers. "Take tonight and sleep on it. We'll discuss this again tomorrow. You'll see things differently in the morning, I'm sure of it."

"I highly doubt it," I said as I pulled away. I hurried outside, with Jake close on my heels.

"Would you like me to drive us home?" Jake offered.

"I can do it," I said. I shook my head and resolved to stop crying, at least until we got back to the cottage.

Jake was silent on the short drive home, and it was so quiet in the Jeep that I heard his stomach rumbling. "I didn't mean to cheat you out of my mother's pot roast."

"I'd rather eat a peanut butter and jelly sandwich with you than dine on the finest meal someplace else alone," he said.

"I appreciate that, and I promise you, giving up Momma's pot roast is the biggest sacrifice I'm ever going to ask you to make."

He was silent for a few more moments before he spoke again. "Suzanne, your mother has to do what's right for her, no matter how hard it is for us to accept. You know that, don't you?"

"Of course I know it," I admitted. "I just don't know what I'm going to do not having her five minutes away from me."

"We could always move there, too," he suggested timidly.

"Jake, I can't take my donut shop with me," I said, "and I'm way too young to retire. So are you, for that matter. You're just on a break, but I know you. You won't be idle for very long. Besides, our lives together are here. This is where most of our friends live."

"I know you have deep roots in the community, and it won't be easy leaving for you, but all I care about is being with you," he said. "Sell the donut shop to Sharon and Emma. We can start another business at the beach if that's what it takes. I don't want to see you miserable, and if you can't see your life without your mother in it, we need to make a change, too."

"You'd really do that for me?" I asked him. I realized for the millionth time that I'd won the lottery when it came to husbands. Though my first choice had turned out to be a dud, the second one had exceeded all expectations.

"I'd walk through fire for you," he said solemnly. "Besides, a move east would get me closer to my sister and her kids in Raleigh. I'd never demand you move for that, but it would be a nice bonus. I'll stay here, or I'll move tomorrow. You just need to decide what you want."

"I don't know what to do," I answered. I'd never even considered the possibility that my mother might not be close by for the rest of my life. Losing my father had been painful enough. In a way, this felt as though I was losing my mother as well. I knew that I'd been spoiled having her nearby for my entire life, but that didn't make me want to be near her any less.

"Why don't you take your mother's advice and sleep on it. She might be right; things might look clearer in the morning."

"I can do that," I said, "but in the meantime, what are we going to feed you tonight? I can't stand the thought of going out to eat and being around other people."

"Why don't I make us something at home?" he suggested.

My husband's specialty was chili, something that a great

many men made, oddly enough, but I didn't think my digestive tract could take it tonight. "I appreciate the offer, but I'm happy to make us something. How about eggs?"

"Could you make me a frittata?" he asked me.

"The fancy kind, or something I just throw together at the last second?" I asked him with a grin. I didn't know how he was doing it, but Jake was getting me outside my own thoughts and the gloom I'd embraced, something I never would have believed possible just a few minutes earlier.

"Your choice. We don't have to even stop at the store, because I know for a fact that there's green pepper in the fridge, two or three kinds of cheese, and maybe a little prosciutto left over from my last sandwich."

"I can make that work," I said. "Are you sure you don't mind eating something so simple?"

"It's not simple to me," he said with a grin. "Plus, there's an added bonus. This way, I get you all to myself, so it's a win-win in my book."

After we ate a delicious meal, there was enough chill in the air that I suggested Jake make a fire while I did a quick cleanup. By the time I came out of the kitchen, he had a nice blaze going.

As my husband patted the couch seat beside him, he said, "Come join me."

"I'd love to," I said.

"We can talk more about it, if you'd like to," he offered.

"Thanks, but there's nothing more to say at the moment. I know I'm being a selfish and spoiled brat, and I hate it, but I already miss my mother, and she hasn't even moved away yet."

"Maybe nothing will come of it," Jake suggested.

"You don't know my mother. Once Momma makes up her mind about something, it's set in stone."

"Okay, then we'll just figure out a way to make the best of it," Jake answered.

"Even if it's selling the donut shop, putting our lovely home on the market, and following her?" I asked him.

"All that is comprised of material things, including Donut Hearts," Jake said. "If I've got you with me, we could be stranded on a desert island and I'd be a happy camper."

"With nothing to eat?" I asked him, forcing a smile.

"Oh, there's plenty to eat on my pretend island."

"And hot running water? You know how I love my shower."

"Of course. We'll have hot water, and a nice restaurant nearby, too."

"I thought this was supposed to be a desert island?" I asked him with a grin.

"It is. Things just magically appear when we want them, but we aren't around other people unless we want to be."

"This is starting to sound more and more like a magical island," I said as I nestled my head onto his shoulder.

"That's exactly what it is. It's whatever we want it to be," he said.

We sat in silence for a while, and before I realized what was happening, I somehow fell asleep.

When I woke up nine hours later, I'd been miraculously transported to our bed. Had Jake picked me up and carried me, or had I awoken and walked into our bedroom half asleep? I was about to ask him which had happened when I noticed that he was gone.

"Jake?" I called out, but there was no response.

I got out of bed, still in my T-shirt and jeans, and padded through the place looking for him.

"There you are," I said when I found him sitting at the kitchen table. He was eating the leftovers from our dinner the night before, and he looked a little guilty as I came in.

"Want some?" Jake asked as he offered the plate to me.

"No, thanks. I'm good," I said as I grabbed a bowl of cereal and joined him.

"How'd you sleep last night?"

"Evidently deeper than I thought. How did I get to bed? Did you carry me there?"

"Not unless I did it in my sleep," Jake said with a grin. "I woke up in the middle of the night and you were gone. I kind of panicked until I found you already in bed. You still had your jeans and T-shirt on, but I didn't want to wake you. After all, you nap in them all of the time, so what could it hurt sleeping in them once?"

"I don't nap all that much," I protested, though I knew that he was right.

"Hey, if I worked your hours, a nap every day would be a requirement. You're off for the next few days, aren't you?"

"It's sweet that you remember my schedule," I said as I took a bite of cereal.

"Are you kidding? I live for your days off. What can I say? I pay attention. That, plus the fact that you write every day off you get in big red letters on our calendar."

"I'd hate to forget and just show up at work one day unexpected," I said. "What's on tap today?"

"I have a few ideas," Jake said. "First of all, I have a question for you, though."

I had a feeling where he was going with that, and I wasn't ready to discuss it. "You can ask me about anything but my mother."

"I wouldn't dare," he said. "My question is, who cleans Teresa's office? I'm assuming she didn't do it herself."

"She has one of my donut customers do it," I said. "Why do you ask?"

"I'm wondering when it was cleaned the last time," Jake said. "I'd love to know how long that label was on the floor, and the red clay dust we found there, too."

"I don't know, but I can call her," I said as I reached for my phone.

"You actually have a customer's number stored in your phone's memory?"

"Every last one of them," I said as seriously as I could manage, and then I laughed. "I'm just kidding. Miranda's husband left her for his secretary a few years ago, and she's got three kids in elementary school. She takes whatever odd jobs she can get around town so she can be there for them when they get out of school. I like to recommend her whenever I can, and when Teresa asked me for some names, I gave her Miranda's."

"That's sweet of you," Jake said.

"Hey, if I can help a friend out, why wouldn't I?" I asked as I dialed Miranda's number.

"You'd be surprised. Not everyone feels that way," Jake said.

"Hey, Suzanne," she said after picking up on the second ring. "Do you have another job for me?"

"No, sorry, it's about something else."

"That's okay. I've got just about all that I can handle at the moment as it is. I was sorry to hear about Teresa Logan, though."

"I know. It's a real shame. You were still cleaning her office for her on a regular basis, weren't you?"

"I took care of it two days ago," Miranda said. "I hate to say it, but I'm glad that my visit wasn't supposed to be *yesterday* morning. I heard that you and your husband found the body. That must have been just awful for you."

"It wasn't fun," I said. "Would you mind if I ask you something while I've got you on the line?"

"Sure, go ahead," she said.

"Did you ever notice anything odd while you were cleaning her office?"

"Like what?" Miranda asked a little cautiously.

"I don't know. Anything out of the ordinary at all, I guess," I answered.

There was quite a long pause before she answered. "Suzanne, I'm grateful for all you do. You know that, don't you?" Miranda asked in a hesitant voice.

"I know that. Listen, if I made you uncomfortable with my question, I take it back. I didn't mean to press you on it."

"No, it's okay. I'm probably just being silly. I just don't want anyone to think I talk out of turn about them. There is one thing that I thought was odd the last time I cleaned for her. It's probably nothing, but it did make me wonder at the time."

"What was it? Remember, you don't have to tell me if you don't want to."

"I found a letter in her trashcan when I was emptying it this week. I wouldn't have dreamed of reading it, but it fell to the floor when I tried to toss it, and when I picked it up, there was something in it that caught my eye."

"Do you by any chance still have it?" I asked her.

"I wish now that I'd kept it. I'm sorry, but it's long gone now."

"Do you remember what it said? What was the gist of it?" I asked.

"It said something like, 'Teresa, you're dead wrong about us. We belong together, and I'm going to make you realize what you're missing, whether you want to face the truth or not. I'm not taking no for an answer, so you might as well give up now. There's only one way this is going to end, and we both know what that is.' I'm not doing it justice. You'd think it was from someone who loved her, but the words just chilled my heart when I read them."

I wished she still had the letter, but maybe there was something else we could learn from it. "Was it signed, by any chance?"

"It just had an A scrawled on the bottom."

"Did you happen to glance at the envelope? I'd love to know if there was a return address, or maybe a postmark."

"I'm sorry. I didn't check. Should I call Chief Grant and tell him about it? I would hate for it to look like I was snooping through the poor woman's garbage just before she was murdered."

"Call him," I said without having to consult Jake. "If it helps the police, you'll be doing Teresa the last favor you could do for her, and if it doesn't matter, the chief won't mind the interruption. Better to err on the side of caution."

"Okay. I'll call him right now. Thank you for the advice."

"Thank you for the information," I said.

I was about to hang up when she asked, "When I call the police chief, should I tell him that we spoke about this?"

I wanted to say no, but I knew that I couldn't do that. It wasn't fair to put that kind of burden on my friend, a woman who had enough weight on her shoulders without me adding to it. "Sure, tell him that we spoke. It's okay with me."

"Thanks. I hate keeping anything from him, you know?"

"I completely understand," I said.

After we hung up, I gave Jake a brief rundown of what Miranda had told me. It was clear that he'd picked a lot of it up just from listening closely. Miranda didn't believe in using her indoor voice, ever, and I was certain that he'd been able to get everything that had been said without my report, but I still felt better giving it.

"That's interesting on so many levels," Jake said after I finished.

"One thing we know for sure is that dust was left there the day she was murdered, and so was the label," I replied. "Miranda's a fierce cleaner. I can vouch for that."

"I'm interested in that, too, but who is this mysterious A?"

"I don't know. Teresa never took me into her confidence, and to be fair, I never asked her about her personal life. Whoever it was, I'm guessing that she rejected him at some point in her life, and he was ready to force his way back into it, no matter what it might take."

"If Miranda's memory is good, it's not exactly a love letter, is it?"

"There seemed to be a lot of implied threats in it, but bear one thing in mind. Miranda went through a pretty nasty divorce, and her view of the men in this world might be a bit tainted," I said. "She gave us her interpretation of that note by memory. It's not something we can take at face value without seeing it for ourselves."

"Maybe not, but we still need to discover who this A character is," Jake said.

"You're right. *Somebody* needs to," I replied, reminding Jake that our investigation was secondary to Chief Grant's inquiry.

"Just not me, right?" Jake asked with a grin.

"Don't worry. There are plenty of other things we can do with our time," I said.

"Like what? I'm open to suggestions."

"Let me grab a quick shower and change my clothes, and I'll see what I can come up with."

CHAPTER 8

"JAKE, WHERE DID YOU GO?" I called out after I took my shower and put on clean clothes. The cottage we shared wasn't that big, but even after I checked out the upstairs where I used to sleep, I still couldn't find him.

Then I noticed that the front door was unlocked. I looked out the window and saw Jake standing on the porch speaking with someone I didn't recognize. It was a man in his late twenties; he was wearing a nice suit, and judging by the BMW in our driveway, he had money and wasn't afraid to spend it. I grabbed my jacket and walked outside to join them.

"Hello, I'm Suzanne," I said as I introduced myself.

"I'm Alexander Rose," he said. "I'm sorry I can't stay and chat, but I really must go. Thank you for the information, Jake."

"Sure thing," my husband said. "Will you be in town long?"

"I'm staying in Union Square at the Marriott," he said. It was the nicest chain hotel within thirty miles of us.

"Good to know," Jake said as Alexander got into his car and drove away.

"What was that all about, and why didn't you invite him in?" I asked Jake as we both stepped back inside the cottage.

"I offered, but he didn't want to stay. He heard that we were the ones who found Teresa Logan's body, and he wanted to hear all about it."

"Did he know her?" I asked.

"According to him, they were engaged at one time," Jake said.

"But not still, right?" I asked incredulously. It was hard to believe that Teresa would have agreed to marry anyone, based on the way she flirted on a wholesale level.

"No. They went to law school together, and he always assumed that they'd get married when they graduated. According to him, that had been the plan all along, but she'd broken it off the night before they marched across the stage to get their diplomas."

"So, he's got to be A. He had to have written the note Miranda found in Teresa's trashcan," I said.

"That's how I figured it, too," Jake said.

"It's kind of odd, him showing up like this right after she's been murdered."

"He told me that he heard the news when he got back to his office, and he took time off work immediately to hurry up here. He admitted to me that he'd been trying to get her back, and he claimed that just when he thought she was warming up to him again, this happened. He seemed heartbroken enough about it."

"Do you believe him?" I asked my husband.

"The truth of the matter is that if Miranda hadn't read that letter and shared its contents with you, I would have completely bought his story. He made a very compelling argument that everything he said was true, and I found myself giving him the benefit of the doubt. He must be one heck of an attorney, I can tell you that much. I'm not that easy to sway."

"Even given what he told you, I'm still not sure why he's here," I said. "What good can possibly come from his presence, even if everything he told you was true?"

"He claims that there's still unfinished business he had with her and that he wouldn't be able to rest until her killer was caught, but I wonder."

When Jake didn't continue, I asked, "What exactly is it that you're wondering? Would you care to share it with me?"

"Sorry. Did I not finish the thought?"

"You did not," I said.

"I've been mulling over one possibility since he first introduced himself. What if he killed her himself?" Jake asked as he frowned.

"Wow, is that always the first place your mind goes?"

"What can I say? I spent too much time in my career questioning the motives of anyone even remotely connected to the case I was working on at the time. Alexander Rose appears to be angry that she was murdered, but it feels a little contrived, if you know what I mean. Maybe he's dealing with it as best he can and my suspicions are based on nothing more than my eagerness to think the worst of people, but I don't completely trust him."

"Could your attitude have anything to do with his chosen profession?" I asked Jake as I took off my jacket.

"Maybe. I've certainly had enough cases snatched away from me at the last second by aggressive attorneys to make me mistrust the lot of them," Jake admitted. "Anyway, he's asked me to keep him informed, and I could swear the man actually tried to pay me for the privilege. When he found out about my background in law enforcement and that I was a private citizen now, he actually asked me if I was for hire, if you can believe that."

"It's not that crazy a concept," I said. "Lots of private detectives are former cops, aren't they?"

"I don't know. I never really thought about it," he admitted.

"Maybe it's something to consider," I said.

"I don't know. I'd have to give it a great deal of thought, and I'm not ready to make that kind of decision right now anyway. There's just too much going on around here at the moment. For at least the foreseeable future, I'm sticking to being an amateur. It's an interesting perspective, to say the least. I thought I had limitations in what I could do before while I was an investigator, but I didn't fully appreciate your constraints until I started working on this investigation with you."

"That's good to know," I said. "It's not always easy, but I don't have to tell you how rewarding it can be when you track down a killer."

"You don't. That's one of the things that gave me the most satisfaction in my former life. Are you ready to hit the ground running this morning?"

"I'm ready if you are," I said.

"Were you able to come up with anything while you were in the shower? I'm at a loss. I'm going to keep my eye on Alexander Rose, but in the meantime, we need something to do."

"As a matter of fact, I did have a thought."

"I want to hear what it is, but first I need to know if it's legal."

"It's fine. It's well within the law. Probably. At least I'm pretty sure that it is."

Jake looked at me for a few seconds before he spoke again. "Maybe you'd better tell me about it before we do anything else that we're going to need to apologize to the police chief for."

"I was thinking that it might not hurt to get a look at Teresa's place and see if there's anything there that might help us," I said. "Surely the chief is finished with it by now."

"You never know, but let's say that he is. We can't just break into the place."

"We don't have to," I said with a smile. "Nick Williams, one of my customers at Donut Hearts, happens to own the house where she was living."

"How could you possibly know that?" Jake asked me in amazement.

"Nick mentioned it when Teresa first came to town, and I filed it away in my mind, along with a hundred thousand other useless facts that I picked up working the front counter of my donut shop every week. Why don't I give him a call?"

"Maybe we should call the chief first and see what he has to say about it," Jake suggested.

"There might not be any need to bother him. If the place is still off limits, Nick will know, and if Stephen has released it, then we should be free to look around there ourselves."

"I really wish you wouldn't call the chief of police by his first name," Jake said with a hint of a frown.

"Why not? I've known him forever, and we've done a ton of things with Grace and him socially. I find it's odd that you keep calling him Chief yourself."

"It's a good way to remind myself that he's the one who's in charge now," Jake said.

"Do you regret turning the job over to him?"

"No, not on your life. I don't ever want to butt heads with you and your mother at the same time about anything ever again," he said.

"Don't forget, Grace and George were in the vehicle that night, too."

"Don't remind me," he said. Jake had been in a position of scolding the four of us at the same time because of some unofficial investigating we were doing without his blessing, and he'd made a decision to resign his temporary position on the spot, though I suspected that he'd been giving it some consideration for some time before that. I hadn't envied him his position, and I'd understood his desire to abdicate it, but it had left a hole in his life, and I was beginning to worry about him. "Just try, for my sake."

"For you, I will," I said. "in my defense, I mostly refer to him as the chief as it is, but I'll refrain from using his name unless it's a social occasion. So, should I call Nick?"

"Go ahead. You might as well see what he has to say," Jake said, so I dialed his number before my husband changed his mind.

"Hey, Nick, it's Suzanne Hart," I said when he picked up the phone.

"I didn't know you sold Donut Hearts," he said unhappily. "When did that happen? If you decide to put the cottage on the market, I'll give you a good price for it. I at least want a shot at it."

"What are you talking about? I still own both places. Why, what have you heard?" The questions were disturbing on a few different levels. Did folks honestly think I was selling everything and leaving town? How had that rumor gotten started? Jake and I had just started talking about it the night before, and as far as I knew, no one else had been privy to the conversation.

"Nothing much really," he said, sounding confused. "It's just that the last two times I bought donuts at your shop, you weren't there. When I tried to ask about it, Emma was too busy to talk. Does that mean that it's not true?"

"Until further notice, I'm here to stay," I said, despite Jake's offer to relocate to wherever Momma and Phillip ended up. I had no idea if I'd take my husband up on his offer, but at the moment, I didn't even want to think about it.

"Okay, that settles that, then," he said. Did he sound a little disappointed hearing the news that I was staying? I honestly didn't want to know, so I didn't ask.

"Teresa Logan rented a place from you when she first came to town, didn't she?"

"She did. It's a cute little house near the hospital. Why, do you know someone who might want to rent it?" he asked eagerly.

I'd almost asked him if Jake and I could snoop around, but I suddenly had a better idea. "I might, but I'd have to see it myself before I could recommend it to my friend. Is it available right now, or do the police still have it sealed off?"

"No, they released it to me ten minutes ago. It's still got all of Teresa's things in it though, and I need to repaint. Give me a week, and I'll be more than happy to show it to you and your friend."

I hesitated before I answered and did my best to sound disappointed. "Sorry, but she's got to move quicker than that. I'm supposed to call her tonight, and there are a few places in Union Square she might be interested in instead." I glanced over at Jake, who was looking at me oddly, which really wasn't all that unusual. I held up an index finger to tell him that I wouldn't be long, and then I continued my conversation with Nick. "Thanks anyway. I'm sorry it didn't work out."

I delayed my hang up long enough for him to stop me, but just barely. "Hold on a second. You can see it now. Suzanne, I can trust you not to take any of her stuff, can't I?"

I wasn't sure that I could make that promise, especially if we found anything that might help our investigation. Summoning up my best righteous indignation, I said loudly, "I can't believe you'd even ask me that. I was going to bring my husband with me. You know, the recent chief of police? If you don't trust me, I'm not sure I want to see it at all now."

"I'm sorry, I don't know what I was thinking. Forget I said anything." He paused a moment. "I'm tied up with something else at this moment, but I can drop off the key on my way. There's a flowerpot on the front porch, so I'll leave it under there. Just lock up and put it back when you're through, and I'll get it later."

"That sounds good to me," I said.

"Don't you even want to know how much the rent is?" he asked me curiously.

I suppose that was a question I should have asked if I'd really had a friend interested in renting the place. "First things first. If I like what I see, then we can discuss money."

"Oh, you'll love it," he said.

"We'll see about that."

After I hung up, Jake asked, "Suzanne, is there something I should know about?"

"What do you mean?"

"Correct me if I'm wrong, but did you just make an appointment to see another place to live, or were you just working an angle to get us in?"

"It's an angle. Trust me, you're not getting rid of me that easily," I said with a laugh.

"That's a relief," he said. "I take it that the place is free now?"

"It will be by the time we get there," I said as I grabbed my Jeep keys. "Come on. I'll drive."

"That's fine with me. I spent so much time on the road driving places alone, it's nice to have someone else chauffeuring me around town."

"Just think of it as part of the service," I said with a grin, "but you'll have to get your own car door. That's where I draw the line."

"I think I can handle that," he replied.

The house was cute, though too small for my taste, and I lived in a fairly modest cottage. If the entire home was four hundred square feet total, I'd be surprised. I knew about the Tiny House movement, but frankly, I had too much stuff to ever be able to do it myself, and that didn't count everything that Jake had. We weren't hoarders by any means, but I couldn't see myself living with so little. I found a great deal of comfort being surrounded by my things, and I admired the people who focused more on living their lives than acquiring more stuff and needing an ever-growing amount of space to store it all in. There had to be a happy medium, at least as far as I was concerned, and I felt as though our cottage maintained a nice balance between necessity and excess. That didn't mean that Jake and I didn't enjoy the television shows that featured the lifestyle, though. Then again, we watched *House Hunters International* and reruns of Julia Child's cooking show, and neither one of us had the desire to live abroad or make gourmet meals. It was entertainment, plain and simple. I loved cozy mysteries that featured recipes to try out myself, but I never seemed to make anything the authors suggested. Honestly, sometimes I enjoyed the descriptions given before the ingredients and directions lists as much as I did the actual mystery.

Teresa had decorated her small space tastefully, with three pieces of art hung on the limited wall space and enough modest furniture to be comfortable in. The bedroom was tiny, but it used every square inch of space to its full advantage, and the kitchen was compact as well. It featured a small oven/cooktop combination that looked more suited for an RV, a tiny sink, and a dishwasher under the counter that couldn't hold enough things from more than one meal at a time. Only the main living space could be considered large, with no internal walls to crowd the space between the kitchen, the dining room, and the living room. Teresa was neat, and everything appeared to have its own place, but that might have been due more to the size of the house than her natural habits.

Jake looked around beside me and whistled softly before he said, "Well, on the plus side, it shouldn't take long to search."

"Could you live like this?" I asked him.

"With you?"

"I wasn't asking you to move out," I said with a smile. "Of course with me."

"Then no."

"How about when you were a bachelor?"

"Again, no," he said. "I need more elbow room."

"I know. They always look bigger on television."

"I don't think so," he said. "So, one of us should take the

kitchen, the other one the bedroom, and we work our way to the middle. What do you think?"

"It sounds like a plan to me," I said. "I'll take the bedroom, if you don't mind."

"Be my guest," he said. "See you in a few minutes."

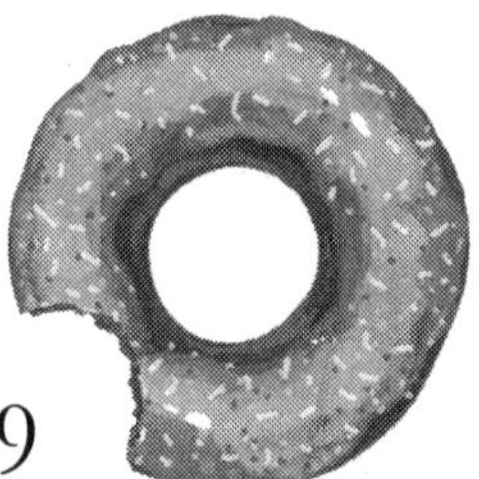

CHAPTER 9

SEARCHING THE BEDROOM TURNED OUT to be a bust, and it didn't take me long to discover the fact. Teresa Logan was neater than I ever would have imagined. Everything had its place, and I wondered if her housekeeping skills were because of the limited amount of space or more because of the meticulous nature of her job. Her shoes were high heeled and polished, her handbags were delicate and tasteful small clutches, and her clothes sported labels that shouted high end. I was beginning to realize that I didn't know much about the woman at all, and I hadn't made much of an effort to find out, either. The fact that she had enjoyed flirting with my husband had tarnished everything else about her to me. It was something hard for me to forgive, especially when she had refused to stop doing it. I began to wonder what might make her act that way. Had she been rejected at an early point in her life, and it had scarred her forever? Perhaps her father had ignored her, and so she kept trying to get the attention of every man she ever met. Could we have been friends under different circumstances? I found myself wondering about her past, but it was too late to learn anything about that now. I'd let one part of Teresa's behavior influence my entire opinion about her. So why was I working so hard to solve her murder now? I knew the answer to that. She'd been working in a space that I owned, and she should have been safe there, but someone had violated that and had killed her in my building. That was what made it so personal. I knew that didn't make much sense logically, but I operated on my emotions as much as I did my intellect. I may not have considered her a friend, but that didn't mean that I was going to turn a blind eye to her murder.

I walked out into the living room and found Jake opening up boxes in the small pantry. "Have you had any luck out here? I pretty much drew a blank in the bedroom," I told him.

"Not yet, but I'm not finished here," Jake said, and then he frowned as he picked up a box of cereal. It was one of the healthy varieties, packed full of fiber and vitamins and all sorts of things that were supposedly good for you. I wouldn't have eaten a bowl of it if it had been the last bit of food in the house.

"What's wrong?"

"There's no way this box should be this heavy," he said.

"Maybe it's all the iron that's packed into it," I said, joking.

Jake opened the box and spilled the contents out onto the small counter.

Something came out of the box, but it wasn't cereal.

It was a personal-sized can of mace, a stun gun, and a receipt.

"Why did she hide that in a cereal box?" I asked as I joined Jake at the counter.

He shook his head as he picked up the receipt and studied it for a moment. "Suzanne, she just bought these things three days ago."

"So, she clearly felt threatened by someone recently. I wish we knew when that letter from A arrived. The timing could be rather telling."

"Is there really any reason not to accept the fact that we're fairly certain who A really is? We both know that Alexander Rose sent it," Jake said.

"I didn't want to jump to conclusions."

My husband shrugged. "Sometimes that's exactly what you have to do. If you don't make certain assumptions, you never get anywhere. My question is, why wasn't she carrying these in her purse when she was attacked?"

"Hang on a second. I think I can answer that question," I said as I walked back into the bedroom. I went straight to her purse collection, and when I looked up, I saw that Jake had followed me into the bedroom.

"What's going on?" he asked as he peered over my shoulder.

"I think I know why Teresa didn't carry the mace or the stun gun. She didn't have a purse large enough to hold them."

"Are you kidding me?" Jake asked.

"See for yourself. Every woman I know has at least one large handbag she carries on occasion, but apparently Teresa was the exception to the rule."

"And it ended up costing her her life," Jake said, shaking his head as he spoke.

"To be fair, she got hit from behind with that bookend. There was no way Teresa could have prevented that, not with what you found, or even if she'd gone out and bought a gun. She literally didn't see it coming."

"That's a fair point," Jake said. "Still, her purchases must mean something. I'm not willing to accept that it was a coincidence that she felt the need for protection, and three days later she was murdered. We need to take this straight to the chief."

"I'm not finished looking around out here," I protested.

"I didn't mean this instant. We might as well be thorough. I'm finished in the kitchen, so it's time we started on the main living space. You take that end, and I'll start over there."

The first thing I did was to glance through the magazines that were neatly arranged on the small coffee table by the most comfortable chair in the place. To my surprise, a small piece of stationery fell out from between two magazines.

I opened it up and read the contents. "Thanks again for dinner. Next time it's on me."

It was signed with a signature familiar to me, Trish Granger, the owner of the Boxcar Grill.

"Did you even know they were friends?" Jake asked me as he leaned over my shoulder. He must have seen me frowning as I read the note and joined me to see what I'd discovered. I hadn't even realized he was behind me.

"I didn't have any idea," I said. "Is there any way this is a clue?"

"To her murder?" Jake asked me, clearly surprised by my question. "Suzanne, you're not accusing Trish of killing Teresa Logan, are you?"

"Of course not," I said. "I'm just wondering if we should show this to St…the chief."

"My guess is that it's probably not relevant," Jake said. "But then again, what could it hurt? It's not as though we're accusing Trish of anything other than sneaking around your back sharing a meal with someone else."

I knew that he'd meant it playfully, but unfortunately, I couldn't bring myself to react that way. "Jake, Trish is welcome to have any friend that she'd like. I do things with Grace all the time without including her, so why should she tell me every last person she shares a meal with when I'm not around?"

"Hey, I was just kidding. Take it easy," he said as he stroked my shoulder lightly. "She probably didn't tell you because she didn't want to upset you. After all, it was no secret to anyone in April Springs about the way you felt about Teresa."

"If Trish knew that I felt that way, then why did she go behind my back and hang out with Teresa?" I asked. Even as I said it, I felt as though I'd reverted to high school again, not a pleasant thing. "I cannot believe how small I just sounded. Forget I said it."

"Why? Suzanne, you're allowed to be petty every now and then, just like the rest of us," Jake said as he hugged me.

The embrace coupled with my husband's acceptance were two parts of the perfect answer to my fit of pique. After a few moments, I broke away from him. "Thank you. I'm all better now. Some things just manage to bring out the worst in me."

"If that's as bad as you ever get, I can find a way to deal with it," he said with a smile.

"That's easy for you to say. I've never seen you react that way to anyone."

"My dear sweet wife, you'd better believe that I have a dark side just as bleak as everyone else."

"If that's really true, then why don't I ever see it?" I asked my husband. It was the complete and unvarnished truth. Jake was rarely angry, and when he was, it was always with good cause. I'd never known the man to be petty about anything.

Jake grinned at me before he answered my question. "It's probably because I keep that part of me chained up in the basement. Every now and then I throw down some food for it, but mostly it stays safely locked up."

"I don't believe you," I said as I kissed him lightly.

"That's your prerogative, but that doesn't make it untrue. Now, let's finish this up and get out of here, shall we?"

"Okay by me."

It didn't take long to finish our search, and nothing out of the ordinary came up over the next ten minutes. We might have missed something, even in that tiny space, but I couldn't imagine what it might be. It would have helped if either one of us had known the woman very well, but as it was, we were there looking for something obvious that anyone would recognize as a legitimate clue. Any nuances about the state of the house would have to be discovered by someone who knew the victim quite a bit better than either one of us had.

"I'm ready to go now if you are," I said. "Before we leave, I wouldn't mind looking around the outside after we lock up. You never know what we might find."

My husband smiled. "I was about to suggest that we do that myself. You're getting pretty good at investigating, Suzanne."

"Really? I'm constantly trying to get better, but sometimes it feels as though the more I know, the more I realize just how much I still need to learn," I admitted.

"In my opinion, that's what makes you good at anything you do." Jake put the things we'd found back into the empty cereal box, added the note from Trish, and then tucked it all under one arm as we exited Teresa's tiny house.

I was just locking the door behind us when I heard someone calling out to us. As I turned, I tucked the key into my front pocket, more as a matter of habit than any planned design.

Alexander Rose trotted toward us. "I'm really glad I caught you," he said, nearly out of breath. Apparently the attorney didn't believe in cardio exercise, not that I did much of that myself.

"What can we do for you?" Jake asked him.

"I just need to get something of mine inside that's important to me. I already spoke with Nick, and he told me that you had the key. I'd appreciate it if you'd let me have it so I can retrieve it and then I'll be on my way."

I made no move to do as he asked. "I'm really sorry, but we can't do that."

The attorney frowned. "I just told you I had the landlord's permission."

"If he wants to let you have the key, you'll need to get it directly from him," Jake said. "However, I'm going to advise him against doing it."

"Why would you do that?"

"You have no right to go in there," Jake said.

"Oh, and you do?" The attorney was clearly getting frustrated by our refusal to do exactly what he wished.

"That's none of your business," Jake said, trying to shut him down.

"We'll just see about that," the attorney said as he turned his back and stormed off. "You're crossing the wrong man."

"It won't be the first time," I said with a smile as he left in a huff.

"You know, he does have a point," Jake said after Rose was gone. "As civilians, we really didn't have any call to be in there any more than he did."

"Maybe not, but do you think Teresa would want him pawing through her things? Miranda told us that she tossed the letter he sent her, but Alexander has no way of knowing that. Is that what he wanted to take, or was he here looking for something else, something that might be even more negative to his reputation than that?"

"If there's anything else hidden in that tiny little space, we certainly couldn't find it," Jake said.

"So, either the police chief has already found what Alexander is after, or Teresa hid it someplace else."

"In her office, perhaps?" Jake asked.

"We've already searched there, and so has Chief Grant," I reminded him.

"True, but as you recall, our search was cut short by the police showing up. Maybe whatever Alexander Rose is looking for is better hidden than any of us realize."

"Should we go back there and look again?" I asked.

"Probably, but not until we see the chief."

"I know, I think it's a good idea, too, but first we're looking around outside, remember?" I asked.

"I'm not about to forget that."

Together, Jake and I walked around the tiny house, and I

was about to give it up as a lost cause when I glanced down into the empty trashcan. There was nothing in it, and I wondered if one of the chief's staff had removed its contents. The tip of something caught my eye on the ground beneath it, and as I lifted up the can, I made a discovery underneath it.

To my surprise, there was a single red rose pressed hard into the ground, or what remained of one. Most of the petals had been ripped off, leaving only a few stragglers in place. The stem was thorny, and as I bent to pick it up, Jake said, "Let me do that." He grabbed his handkerchief and retrieved it for me.

"What do you suppose that means?" he asked me as he studied it.

"Well, a single red rose usually means I love you," I said. "Evidently, Teresa wasn't too pleased to get the message from whoever sent it, based on the condition of this. It's barely more than a stem."

"Why was it under the can, though?" Jake asked.

"Maybe tossing it inside just wasn't good enough."

"Or maybe she threw it and missed, and when the police team emptied the trashcan, they inadvertently covered up what might be evidence."

"That's probably more likely," I said. "Do you think that was what Alexander Rose was just looking for? Hey, that makes sense. A man named Rose would absolutely give the woman he's stalking a single red rose."

"It's got a certain poetic ring to it, but it might not be that obvious a connection," Jake said. "After all, he claims he just got into town, and based on the condition of what's left of this flower, this happened at least a few days ago."

"I agree, but only if we can trust him when he told us that he just showed up," I said.

"True. Then again, it could have come from Bobby Wells declaring his undying love."

"As long as you didn't send it, we're good," I said.

"Take my word for it. It didn't come from me," Jake replied.

"Then let's go show this to the chief, too."

Fortunately, Chief Grant was in his office. It was taking some time to call him that, but I knew that it was important to do it, and not just for my husband's sake. Stephen Grant had earned the title, and I was going to use it from now on, at least when he was working in his official capacity.

"Hello, Chief," Jake said as we walked into his office with our discoveries. "Do you have a minute?"

"Of course. What have we got?" the chief asked as he cleared off a place on his desk after seeing the cereal box in my husband's hand.

Jake pulled out the stun gun, the mace, and the receipt first. Chief Grant studied them each in turn, and then he frowned as he looked at Jake. "Do you mind if I asked you where you found these?"

"They were in a cereal box in Teresa Logan's pantry," he admitted.

"That area was supposed to have been checked," the chief said, clearly unhappy with our discovery.

"Be that as it may, we thought that it was important to bring everything we found in her rental to your attention."

"I appreciate that," he said as he moved the objects off to one side. "Was that all that you found?"

"No, but I have a question for you first. Did you realize that Trish Granger and Teresa Logan were friends?"

"We knew about that, yes," the chief said, looking uncomfortable as he admitted it.

I showed him the note. "Then this won't come as a surprise to you."

He glanced at it, and then he said, "We considered it

insignificant. Do you have any reason to suspect that it's tied into the murder?"

"No, of course not. Out of curiosity, did Grace know, too?" I asked him. "I'm not asking you as the police chief, I'm asking you as her boyfriend."

"You'll have to direct that question to her," the chief replied, refusing to make eye contact with me.

"So the answer is yes, then," I said, biting my lip. Why had my best friend kept that particular bit of news from me? It wasn't like Grace, and I was disappointed in her.

He took a deep breath, and then let it out slowly before he spoke. "Suzanne, as far as I know, Grace wasn't aware of the friendship any more than you were. The only reason I know about it at all is because I read that note. Don't you think she would have told you if she'd realized it?"

"Yes," I said, suddenly asking Grace for forgiveness for jumping to the wrong conclusion, though I'd never voiced it to her. "You don't suspect Trish of killing Teresa Logan, do you?"

"No. The two of us had a conversation about their relationship earlier, and I'm satisfied with her answers. She's pretty torn up about it, to be honest with you. It's never easy losing a friend, especially if she feels she has to hide it from others she cares about."

I suddenly realized that I hadn't made it easy for Trish to share her burden with me. I doubted that her tears had been generated because of onions, though knowing Trish, she'd probably pitched in by chopping them to give herself a reasonable excuse for her crying. I needed to make it a priority to talk to her and clear the air between us; I hated the thought there were any secrets between us. She should be able to tell me anything, and vice versa.

"What about this?" Jake asked him as he presented the remnants of the rose we'd found out back.

"We didn't find that, either. Where was it?"

"Under the trashcan," I said. "It was easy to miss." I felt bad about ratting out one of the chief's officers, but he needed to know what we'd found.

"It's nice of you to try to cover for my people, but you found it, didn't you?"

"That's only because I was working with a highly trained professional," I said with a smile, trying to ease the blow of our discovery.

"You're the one who found it, Suzanne," Jake corrected me. "Chief, you should know that as we were leaving the property, Alexander Rose showed up and tried to get us to let him into Teresa's place. He claimed that there was something of his inside."

"What did you do?"

"We refused to let him in," I said as I slid the key across the desk to him. "Maybe someone should pack her things up for her next of kin before someone else goes through it all."

"I'll have one of my people do it," he said, "and I know just who to have handle it."

There was no doubt in my mind that whoever had missed the cereal stash and the rose was going to be spending the rest of the day going through Teresa Logan's things again, not that I could blame the chief. A pair of valuable clues had been missed, so a lesson needed to be learned.

"If we accept Alexander Rose's statement that he just got here as legitimate and he didn't bring her the rose, then who might have?" I asked him. I had my own suspicions, but I wanted the chief to reveal his first.

"It could be any secret admirer," the chief admitted.

So much for that line of questioning. "Or a not-so-secret one. Bobby Wells could have done it."

"It sounds like something he'd do," the chief agreed. "I'll ask him."

"And if he denies it?" I asked Chief Grant.

"Then we'll add it to the list of things that don't make any sense at the moment. Was there anything else you needed to bring to my attention?"

"That's all that we've been able to uncover so far. Will it do us any good to ask you how your end of the investigation is going?"

"It's slow slogging right now," the chief admitted. "I'm going to visit Joe Chastain and Becky Rusch again, but I'm not sure that we've got anything to ask them that we didn't ask before. There's some physical evidence that we're still working on, but Jake, you know how cases like this go sometimes. It takes awhile to gather all of the pertinent information."

"Have you had any luck with the voice on the answering machine?" I asked, blurting it out before remembering that the police chief had no way of knowing that we'd heard that until I'd just admitted it to him.

"Why am I not surprised you played the tape," he said.

"In our defense, we didn't touch the button with a finger, nor did we erase it after we heard it. The blinking light on the machine was too much to just ignore," Jake said.

The chief seemed to accept that. "We don't know who left it, but we're going through her case files to try to determine who might have had a grudge against her. Teresa was ruthless when she went after someone, and I'm seeing a side to her that I hadn't seen before. She had a tendency to use a hammer when a feather would do, if you know what I mean."

"You don't have to tell that to me," I said, remembering her throwing herself at my husband shortly before she was murdered.

"Is there anything else you two are keeping from me?" the chief asked after a prolonged sigh.

"No, we've told you everything," I said.

"Jake?" he asked my husband.

"What, my word suddenly isn't good enough for you?" I asked indignantly.

"Suzanne, we both know that it's a fair question for me to answer," my husband said calmly. He turned to the chief. "You know everything that we know."

"I was afraid of that," the chief answered. "I was hoping you were still holding something good out on me."

"No such luck," Jake answered with a chuckle. I didn't find any of it particularly funny, but evidently Jake hadn't had a problem with it, so why should I? After all, he was the former professional law enforcement officer, and I was just an amateur at this line of work.

"Well, anything you do uncover, I'd appreciate a heads-up," Chief Grant said.

"Do you mind telling us if Joe Chastain was telling the truth about Teresa making a call around eight thirty the night she was murdered? Surely you've checked her phone records by now." I probably shouldn't have asked the question, but my pride was still stinging a little.

"She called her college roommate," the chief admitted. Maybe he felt a little bad about the way he'd treated me. I wasn't above accepting a pity clue.

"Did she mention anything that might help?" I asked him.

"No, they were making plans to go to a friend's wedding," he said. "She was torn up to hear about Teresa's murder." After a moment of silence, he leaned forward and grabbed his phone. "Send Winston in. I have a job for him."

It was our cue to leave, and Jake and I didn't have to be told twice.

Once we were back outside, Jake said, "You know I didn't mean anything earlier, don't you?"

"We're good," I said with a smile. The information the police chief had shared with us had eased my ire quite a bit, and there was no use being upset about the implication that I might be holding something back, especially since I'd done just that a time or two in the past.

"Thanks," Jake said. He looked relieved by my reaction. "Should we go back and check out Teresa's office again?"

"That sounds good, but there's a stop we need to make first."

"Let me guess. We're going to the Boxcar, aren't we?" Jake asked.

"I want to talk to Trish."

"Suzanne, you can't hold her choice of friends against her, especially when she's grieving for one of them."

I stared at him for a second before I spoke. "Is that really what you think I'm going to do? I want to offer a dear friend my sympathy for her loss. That's it."

"I'm sorry. I should have known better. I seem to keep stumbling over my own words today. You know I think you're wonderful, right? The truth is, I aspire to have the loyalty to my friends that you have to yours. I never meant to imply otherwise."

I suddenly felt sorry about upbraiding him like that. After all, I knew that Jake had only my best interests at heart. "It's fine. I guess I'm just a little sensitive at the moment."

"It's completely understandable," Jake said. "Would you like me to go in with you?"

"If you wouldn't mind, I really need to do this alone. No offense intended."

"None taken," he said. "Why don't you put the Jeep in the Boxcar parking lot, and I'll walk over to the crime scene while you're talking to Trish. You can catch up with me when you're finished."

"I'd rather we go over there together, if you don't mind," I said. "I don't like the idea of you investigating by yourself."

"Suzanne, I was a state police investigator for more years than I like to think about. I can handle myself in a pinch," he said with a gentle smile.

"I know that, but if something *does* happen to you, I want to be right there beside you. Humor me, okay?"

"Fine. I suppose I could run home while you're talking with Trish. Maybe I could grab a snack while I'm there. Is there any pie, by any chance?"

I laughed. "You know as well as I do that there isn't, but I'll bring you a slice from Trish's while I'm there. What kind would you like?"

"I don't know. Surprise me," he said with a grin.

After we drove over to the Boxcar, I parked my Jeep and Jake and I parted ways. As he walked through the park toward home, I took a deep breath and walked up the steps to the grill so Trish and I could have a little talk. It was time to clear the air between us and to offer my sympathy for her loss. I hadn't been a member of Teresa Logan's fan club, but that didn't mean that I couldn't offer comfort to one of my dearest friends because of her loss.

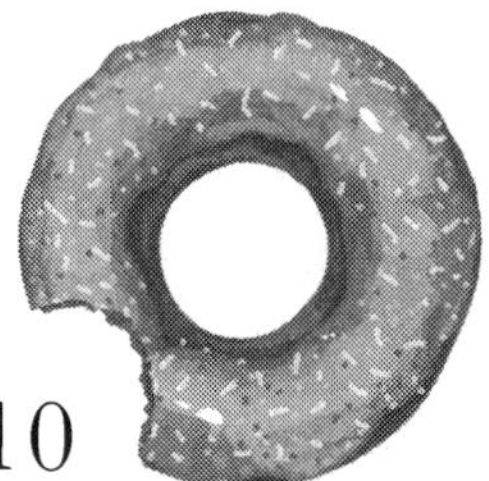

CHAPTER 10

"HEY, TRISH. DO YOU HAVE a second?" I asked as I approached the register at the Boxcar Grill.

She looked surprised to see me again. "Back so soon? Did you change your mind about that pie after all?"

"As a matter of fact, we did, but that's not the only reason I'm here. Is there someplace we can talk in private?"

Trish looked at me quizzically for a moment, and then she glanced around at the nearly empty grill. "Sure, why not? Come on back."

I was one of the rare folks who had been invited back into the inner sanctum where the food was prepared at the Boxcar. While the dining area was made up of one long boxcar, the kitchen was another, attached side by side via a method that I didn't fully understand. I smiled and waved to Hilda, who was busy working at the grill, but she managed to nod at me and look concerned toward her boss at the same time. She made a gesture with her spatula that told me I needed to do something about that, and in truth, it was the real reason that I was there.

As Trish grabbed a box for our pie, she asked, "What kind would he like? I'm assuming this is for your husband."

"It wasn't that hard to guess, was it?" I said with a grin. "Do you have any peanut butter and chocolate left?" It was one of Jake's favorites, a special treat that he really loved. The crust was made up from crushed chocolate cookies, sugar, and butter, while the top mixture definitely had peanut butter in it, and whipped cream, too, along with other ingredients I couldn't begin to guess at. I'd have to get the recipe from her sometime, but I had more important things to talk to her about at the moment.

"There's two pieces left. Why don't we send one home with you for Jake, and we can split the other one while we chat? I'll risk the calories if you will."

She didn't have to twist my arm. "It's a deal."

"Good. I've been needing something decadent today," she said. It was the opening I needed, and I wasn't going to let it just pass.

"That's why I'm here." After Jake's piece was safely put away, Trish transferred the last piece to a plate, and then she produced a pair of forks. I took my first bite and sighed happily. "That's every bit as good as I remember it."

"It should be. We haven't changed a thing about the recipe since we first opened."

"The reason I came by is because I just found out about something. I'm sorry you lost your friend yesterday," I said quietly after my next bite.

"What are you talking about?" Trish asked me haltingly, a large chunk of pie dangling precariously on the edge of her fork as she stared at me.

"I know that you were friends with Teresa Logan," I said. "It's tough losing someone you care about. Trish, you didn't have to hide it from me. We don't have to have the exact same set of friends. Just because someone isn't one of my favorite people in the world is no reason you shouldn't make your own decisions about them."

"I understand that, but I knew how you felt about her, Suzanne. Believe me, I tried talking to her about how she acted around Jake, but she wouldn't listen. I know you don't want to hear this, but she was usually a sweet woman, and a nice person to hang out with, despite her propensity to flirt with any man in pants. The truth is that her father left her mother right after Teresa was born. Added to that, she never got much attention in high school or college from men. According to her, she was a real ugly duckling, but she blossomed in law school, and suddenly she couldn't get enough of the attention that she'd always craved but never received. She was actually engaged to a fellow student in law school, but she knew it wasn't going to work out, so she broke it off with him right before they graduated. She just wasn't ready to settle down, not with him, or anyone else, for that matter. I know it doesn't excuse her behavior, but it does explain it, at least a little bit."

The truth was that up until Jake and I had stumbled across her dead body the day before, I'd never looked at the situation from Teresa's point of view. She had been one of the bad guys in my eyes. Someone in my book club had once made the point that everyone is the hero of their own story, even the villain, and I'd found that it was an interesting way of looking at people in real life, too. That didn't mean that I condoned the attempted stolen kiss from my husband, but really, how could I blame her, given her history? Would I be any different if our circumstances had been the same? Besides, Jake was charming, nice looking, and he had an air of politeness and intensity about him that some women took the wrong way. I felt badly about the way I'd treated Teresa while she'd been alive, but there was nothing I could do about that now except help my husband find her killer. "I'm sorry that you couldn't say something to me before, but I realize now that it was my problem, not yours," I said. "I didn't mean for it to ever be awkward between us."

Trish hugged me. "I'm sorry I kept it from you."

"The way I've been acting, I can't even blame you for doing it," I said. "Are we okay?"

"Yes. I feel so much better. I couldn't stand keeping something like this from you."

We were both blubbering at that point, but in a good way, and after a full minute, we broke apart, each of us now smiling. If Jake had been watching the exchange, he would have thought that we'd both lost our minds, but Hilda nodded and smiled as she watched it all transpire.

"I'm glad we had this chat," I said.

"I am, too," she replied as she dabbed at her eyes.

"Excellent. Then we're all set. Jake and I are doing our very best to figure out who killed Teresa. You know that, don't you?"

"I hoped you were," Trish said. "Is there anything I can do to help?"

"That depends. Do you know anything that might be of use to us?"

Trish frowned for a moment, and then she said, "That's a hard question to answer, isn't it? Besides, I'm not sure how I feel about talking about this with you."

"It's only going to be uncomfortable if we choose to let it be," I said.

"You're right. There's probably something you should know, but I'm not sure how you're going to take it."

"Try me. I just might surprise you," I said.

"There's a reason Teresa tried to kiss Jake when she did. She finally took my advice and asked someone more age appropriate out on a date, but he rejected her. She reacted badly, and Jake happened along at exactly the wrong time when she was as fragile as I'd ever seen her."

"Do you know the name of the man she asked out? Was it someone here in town?" I couldn't imagine who it might be.

"No, he lives in Hickory. I'm guessing that you don't know him, but that's kind of beside the point. He doesn't figure into this. Teresa's been feeling vulnerable lately anyway, and she was trying to get more control of her life. The thing is, there was someone around here that she has been afraid of for a few weeks, but I could never get a name out of her."

"Is that why she bought the mace and the stun gun?" I asked her.

"Did she actually go ahead and do that?" Trish asked me. "Teresa promised me that she was going to, but I didn't know that she had done it yet. If she had a few things for self-defense, why didn't she use them on her attacker? They might have saved her life."

"My guess is that part of the reason is that it's something as simple as not having a big enough handbag to carry them around in," I said, sharing my recent observation with her.

Trish frowned for a moment before she spoke again. "That makes sense. We were going to go shopping this weekend in Charlotte, and she said that buying a bigger purse was the first thing on her list."

"If it's any consolation, it appears that the attack was sudden and unexpected. I'm not at all sure the mace or the stun gun would have done her any good."

"How can you possibly know that?" Trish asked. We'd both completely forgotten about the peanut butter pie, which was hard to believe given the way we felt about treats.

"From the look of things at the crime scene, Teresa most likely never even saw it coming. She was hit from behind before she even had the time to turn around. Is there anyone you can think of who might want to harm her, and yet she'd still feel safe enough to turn her back on?"

"I wish I had a list of names for you, but I have no idea," Trish said. "Even if it were someone she didn't fully trust, how much trouble would it be for them to wait until she reached to get something or even heard a noise and turned to see what it might be without giving it any thought?"

"I just wish we had a name," I said.

"If I had to make a list, I'd put Alex Rose's name on it, but he doesn't live around here."

"That doesn't mean he's in the clear. He's in town, and I've spoken with him twice in the past twenty-four hours," I said.

"You're kidding. How did you happen to run across his path?"

"First, he came by the cottage this morning to speak with Jake, and then, a little bit ago, he tried to get into Teresa's house while Jake and I were there."

"You were at her place? Why?"

"I told you before. We're investigating her murder," I said.

"And the police just let you in?"

"Not exactly." I explained my little white lie that had gained us access. I was expecting disapproval, but she didn't seem to mind, maybe because it had been done for a good cause.

"Did you find anything?"

"Jake found the mace and the stun gun, along with the receipt for them, in an empty cereal box in the pantry," I said, "but I already told you that."

"What else did you find?" It was clearly painful for Trish to hear these things, but I didn't have any right not to share them with her.

There was no way around telling her what else we'd uncovered. "We found your note thanking her for dinner," I admitted, feeling like some kind of peeping tom for some odd reason. "That's how I found out you two were friends."

"I'd like to have that back, if I may." Trish was doing a remarkable job of holding it together, and I wished with all my heart that I could satisfy her request, but I couldn't.

"I'm so sorry, but the police chief has it," it pained me to admit.

"That makes sense. Why wouldn't you turn it over to him?" Trish paused a moment in thought, and then she asked,

"Suzanne, you don't think that I had anything to do with what happened to Teresa, do you?"

"Of course not," I said quickly, and I meant it. "Jake and I were just being thorough. Don't blame him for that, either. His training runs pretty deep."

"I get it. Was there anything else?"

"There was one more thing that was kind of odd. We found the stem of a single rose under the trashcan out back. The petals had mostly been destroyed, but it was clear that's what it was."

After Trish took all of that in, she said, "You said that Alex showed up while you were there. Suzanne, please tell me that you didn't let him inside her place. Teresa would have hated the thought of Alex Rose pawing through her things."

"No, we refused to do it, and he stormed off in a snit. We turned the key over to Chief Grant, and he's having one of his officers pack up Teresa's things even as we speak."

"I should be the one who does that," Trish said. "After all, I was just about her only friend in town. She deserves at least that much."

"Does she have any family left that you know of?" I asked her.

"No, they're all gone from what she told me. For all intents and purposes, she was alone in the world. I'm calling Stephen. He's got to let me do this. It's important."

I didn't correct her use of his first name and not his title. After all, Trish could call the police chief whatever she chose to. I toyed with my fork as she talked, but I didn't take another bite. I'd lost my appetite, even for something as delicious as that pie.

When she hung up, she looked at me and nodded. "Okay, I'm meeting the officer as soon as I can get over there. Thank you for letting me know what was going on."

"I'm just sorry I couldn't do more."

"Find the killer," she said intently as she grabbed her handbag. "That's all I need."

"Who else should we be looking at besides Alexander Rose?" I asked her before she could go.

"Talk to her client list. She had some pretty bad eggs she dealt with on a regular basis. She couldn't go into specific details, but there were some rough customers."

"We've already got Joe Chastain and Becky Rusch on our list. Anyone else?"

She paused a moment, and then she said, "Do you know about Bobby Wells? He's been stalking her for awhile."

"We've spoken with him, and so have the police."

Trish frowned for a moment, and then she said, "That's about all I can think of. Listen, I need to get over to Teresa's place."

"Understood. Let me pay you for the two slices of pie."

"They're on the house," she said.

"You don't have to do that."

"I know, but I want to."

"Can I hang around and help run the place while you're gone?" I offered. "I can run the register and wait tables, and I'm sure Jake would be happy to clean the tables." I didn't hesitate offering our services. It was for a friend, and I knew that Trish would gladly do the same thing for me.

"You're sweet to offer, but I've got it covered." She called out, "Hilda, I'll be gone for about an hour. Do me a favor and call Gladys, would you? She'll be glad to come by and help out, but until she gets here, the place is all yours."

Trish hurried out the back, probably because that was where she was parked, so I grabbed Jake's piece of pie and headed out the front door myself.

I was two steps from making it when I heard an angry voice in the background behind me, arguing about a basketball game that he'd watched the night before.

I instantly knew that this was the same voice Jake and I had heard on Teresa's answering machine, threatening her just before she'd been murdered, so I turned to the few folks there in search of our mystery suspect.

"Hey, Burt. Do you have a second?"

"Hello, Suzanne," Burt Gentry, the owner of the hardware store, said when he saw me approach. It was odd to see a man with red hair that tan, especially this time of year. "What do you need? I'm busy at the moment."

"Fine. When you get a chance, I need a word with you." Taking a page out of my husband's interrogation book, I just stood there.

He tried to ignore me, but Arthur Bradshaw finally said, "For goodness sake, give the girl two minutes. Your time's not worth that much, and you know it."

"Fine," Burt said, frowning as he stood and faced me. "Make it quick. I've got to pick Marge up pretty soon."

"I can wrap it up with one question. Why did you threaten Teresa Logan on her answering machine the night she died?"

"Would you keep your voice down?" Burt said as he grabbed my arm and walked me up front to where no one was currently standing.

I let him lead me, trying my best not to smile. It appeared that I'd finally managed to get his full attention. "Now, what is this nonsense that you are talking about?"

"Don't try to deny it, Burt. I heard the message, and so did the police chief. The second I leave here, I'm telling him that it was you."

"I don't know what you're talking about," he said, doing his best to bully me into backing down.

I knew he was bluffing, but he wasn't counting on me calling him on it. Besides, I had something that would shake his denials to the core.

I pulled out my phone and replayed the message for him.

When he heard the first part of it, "Do you think you can bully me?" in his own voice, Burt made a grab for my phone, but I was too quick for him. I thought about letting it play on, but then I decided that I'd rather get the truth than embarrass him.

He looked mad enough to spit fire. "I said stop that blasted thing."

I'd already killed it, so I smiled at him sweetly as I asked, "Are you saying that you remember leaving the message now?"

"Of course I remember it," he said. "I left it right before our ship left port."

"Where did you go?"

"I took my wife on a short cruise, if you must know. We got back an hour ago, and I just heard about Teresa Logan."

"I suppose you can prove that," I said.

"You bet I can. I have the ticket stubs, our receipt for the cruise, and about a thousand witnesses who can verify that I was on board the entire time. Now I don't know how you got hold of that tape, but you'd better erase it right now, or I'm going to be calling my lawyer. It's already going to be a mess straightening out all of the chaos that blasted Logan woman was causing me, so I can't imagine it would cost me that much more to sue you while I'm at it."

If Burt was telling the truth, there was no point in me having a copy of that voicemail message, and if he wasn't, I knew that Chief Grant would find out soon enough. I did as he asked and erased the message, and then I smiled. "There you go. It's gone."

"Why should I believe you?"

"Because I'm telling the truth," I said. "If you don't trust me, then go ahead and sue me. I bet my mother's attorneys can embarrass yours, but if you want to find out, I'm ready and willing."

He didn't have an answer for that.

I walked out with Jake's pie, but before I went back to the cottage, I called the chief of police along the way. "Hi, Chief," I said when he picked up.

"Suzanne, you can call me Stephen if you'd like."

"No, sir, as a matter of fact, I can't. Jake explained to me that you're the chief now, and you deserve the respect that title carries with it."

"Does that mean you won't ever call me by my first name again?" he asked, sounding amused and resigned to the fact all at the same time.

"If we all go out on a double date, then you'll be Stephen."

"How about if I come into the donut shop for a treat?"

"That depends. Are we talking about your day off?" I asked him.

He paused. "Sure, let's say that it's my day off."

"In that case, it will still be Chief."

He laughed. "Thanks, I needed that. Is there something I can do for you, or are you just calling to make me smile?"

"There's something you need to know. I just discovered the name of the mystery man who left a message on Teresa Logan's answering machine."

"How did you manage that? I've still got the state investigators tracking that down for me."

"I got lucky. I was at the Boxcar and I overheard Burt Gentry arguing with some of his friends, and the moment I heard him raise his voice, I knew that it was him."

"Burt! I knew I'd heard that voice before. Don't say anything to him, okay? I'll be right there."

"There might be a problem with that," I said hesitantly.

"You already spoke to him about it, didn't you?"

"I'm sorry. I did," I said.

With a resigned voice, he asked, "What did he say?"

"He and Marge took one of those short two day–one night

cruises, and he swears that they just got back into town. He claims that he made the call, got on the ship, and then he was on it the time of the murder."

"Do you believe him?"

"Sadly, I do. I was hoping that he'd lie to me, but he seemed pretty confident that his alibi would hold up, so I don't think he's involved with what happened to Teresa Logan."

"I'm surprised that he confessed that he left the message to you," the chief said. "How did you manage that?"

"I might have taped it off the machine when we first heard it and then played it back for him to give him a little nudge," I admitted.

"You *might* have?"

"Okay, that's exactly what I did. I didn't figure it could hurt anything, and it might help to have the exact words on tape for further review. If it's any consolation, I just erased it, so you have the only copy. You don't mind, do you?"

"What good would it do me to say that I do now?"

"You're a good guy. I knew you'd understand," I said. "Oh, by the way, thanks for letting Trish handle packing up Teresa's things. That was sweet of you."

"I had ulterior motives," he said. "As Teresa's friend, she might notice something that shouldn't be there or, just as importantly, something that's missing that should be."

I didn't tell him that I'd had that exact same thought. "So, are you claiming that your charitable good deed was just a way to do your job better?" I asked him.

"That's what it's going to show in the report I file later, anyway," he said with a chuckle. "Do you have any more blockbusters for me at the moment?"

"Not just yet, but we're still working on it."

"With all that you and Jake are accomplishing, I'm not sure why I shouldn't just close up the office and go on a cruise myself," the chief said with a hint of humor in his voice.

"We both know that you'd never do that while Grace was out of town."

"There are a great many reasons it's not happening, not just my girlfriend's absence," he said. "Thanks for letting me know about Burt."

"You'll verify his alibi, just in case?" I asked.

"The minute we hang up," Chief Grant said, and then he did just that.

As I was putting my cell phone away, I looked up from the parking lot to see my husband walking toward me.

"Is that pie?" he asked.

"It is. I thought you were going to wait for me at home."

"I got bored," he said with a grin. "I don't suppose there's a fork in there, is there? If there isn't, it's not going to be a problem. I've been known to use my fingers before, and I'll do it again if it's needed."

"You don't have to remind me. Let's see." I popped open the container and saw that Trish had indeed included a plastic utensil. "You're in luck."

He took it from me, and then frowned. "We have a problem."

"What's that? You still like peanut butter and chocolate pie, don't you?"

"Of course I do, but there's only one fork here."

"That's because you don't have to share your piece. It's all yours."

My husband looked at me as though I'd just given him a hundred-dollar bill. "Seriously?"

"Seriously. That's just the kind of woman you married."

"You already had some, didn't you?" he asked suspiciously.

"Part of one, but that doesn't make my sacrifice any less meaningful."

"Agreed. You can still have some if you want."

I couldn't bear to deprive him of the smallest bite, and I told him so.

He didn't fight me on it.

After Jake sat on a nearby bench, I brought him up to speed on what I'd uncovered as he ate.

"So, Burt Gentry left that message. It figures. I really don't like that man," Jake said.

"I don't, either," I agreed. "But apparently he's not a killer. Where does that leave us?"

"With one less suspect," my husband said as he happily ate his piece of peanut butter and chocolate pie. "Right now, we're still looking at Joe Chastain, Becky Rusch, Bobby Wells, and Alexander Rose. I don't know about you, but after we explore Teresa's office again, if we don't find anything else compelling, I say we go after the first two again. Maybe now that they've had a little time to stew, they could be a little more pliable."

"I don't see how, but I'm willing to speak with them again if you are."

Jake ate quite a bit more, and then he handed me the container.

"There's still more pie here," I protested.

"It's for you. Consider it a reward for your earlier self-sacrifice."

"Are you sure? Don't make me an offer you're not willing to back up."

"I'm positive," he said.

I promptly ate the last two bites. "Thanks. Now, let's drive over to the office to see if we can unearth another clue."

Evidently someone had beaten us to it, though.

The front door was busted wide open and was swinging gently in the breeze.

It appeared that someone had taken it upon themselves to do a little searching themselves, and I wondered what we would find there or if they'd uncovered something that we'd missed.

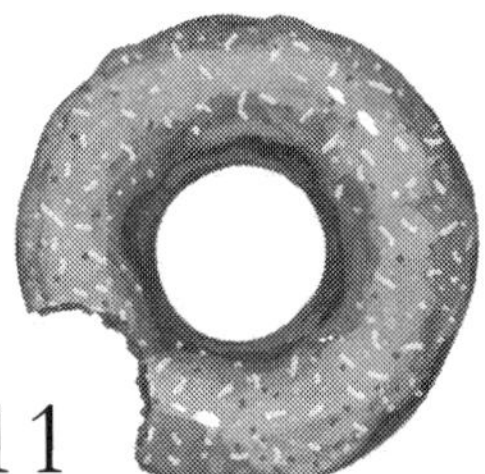

CHAPTER 11

I STARTED TO GO IN WHEN Jake put a hand on my arm.

"What's going on? We need to check this out." I said.

"Suzanne, I'm not the police chief anymore, remember? What if someone's still inside?"

"Then you'll handle them," I said.

"I appreciate your vote of confidence, but we're still calling the chief." Jake took out his phone and called Chief Grant. "Bishop here. We're at Teresa Logan's office, and it looks as though someone has just broken in."

After a moment of conversation from the other end, Jake hung up. "He's on his way."

The chief was as good as his word, because thirty seconds later, we saw a patrol car screaming up the road toward us. "I guess he was close by," Jake said with a grin.

Chief Grant got out of the cruiser and drew his gun. "Stay right here. I'll be back."

"Do you want some backup?" Jake offered.

"Are you armed?"

"No," my husband admitted.

"Then wait for me."

We both did as we were told. "I thought you always carried a weapon on you," I said.

"I usually do, but I'm trying to break the habit," he said. "After all, I'm not a cop anymore. I'm just a private citizen like everybody else."

"There's no way on earth you're like everybody else. Do me a favor. While we're investigating a murder, start carrying a weapon again."

"I didn't think you approved of me going around armed," he said.

"What makes you say that?"

"I don't know. It's just the general impression I've gotten."

I shook my head. "The truth is that I'm not sure that I have an opinion one way or the other, but I do know that there have been times in the past when being armed might have made the difference between life and death."

"Why don't you carry one, then?" he asked me. "A concealed carry permit isn't that tough to get."

"I'd probably end up shooting my own foot, or worse yet, having someone take it away from me. You've been highly trained, though. It's not the same thing at all."

"That's probably a fair point. Here he comes," Jake said as the police chief came out, his gun now holstered. "It's all clear."

"Did they get all of Teresa's files?" I asked.

"No, I had them removed yesterday. I had a feeling someone else might want to see something inside one of them," he said with a smile. "I'm afraid you're going to have to replace the lock, and maybe even the door jamb, too," he told me. "It appears as though someone kicked it in."

"Isn't that hard to do? The reason I'm asking is I'm wondering if it means that someone strong did it."

"Jake, do you want to handle that question?" the chief asked.

"No, it's more about technique than it is brute strength. As far as I'm concerned, any one of our suspects could have done it," he told me. "Should I call someone about fixing the lock?"

"That can wait for the moment," I said, and then I turned to the chief and asked, "How bad is the rest of it?" I envisioned mass chaos inside, and I wasn't looking forward to cleaning it up.

"Besides the broken lock, you'd never know that anyone broke into the place. My guess is whoever did this saw that the files were gone and took off."

"So it could have just been a disgruntled client and not a killer," I said.

"There are quite a few reasons someone could have broken in, and some of them might not have been related to the murder at all. I don't think they'll be back, so you should be fine for the moment," the chief said, "I'd get that door fixed sooner rather than later if I were you." He turned to Jake before he left. "Thanks for not just barging in and calling me so I could handle this. I appreciate that."

"Hey, you're the police chief," Jake said with a grin. "I'm just an innocent bystander."

"I don't know that I'd call you particularly innocent," I said as I waved good-bye to the police chief and thanked him for coming.

After he was gone, we walked inside, and Jake studied the lock and frame on the way in. "I can probably fix this. I just need to run by the cottage and grab some tools first."

"That can wait," I said. "I want to have a good look around before anything else happens here."

"You heard the chief. Nothing else was taken."

"That he knows of," I said. "Do you believe this was just a coincidence?"

"No, but to be fair, I doubt that he does, either."

"Then why did he just imply that?" I asked.

"He probably wanted to give you a little reassurance that whoever did it probably isn't coming back."

"Do you believe that?"

"I do. Either they found what they wanted, or they realized it was already gone. Either way, we should be okay once we get that door fixed."

"Then let's go in and see if everybody's been missing something," I said.

"If they have, what are the odds of us finding it?" Jake asked me.

"I'll admit that they aren't very good, but that's not going to stop me from searching the place."

"Lead on," he said.

We walked into the office together, and I started looking around for anything that might be out of place or missing, but nothing caught my eye immediately. After twenty minutes, I knew that I could have stood there all day and not come up with anything. If there was a clue still here, I wasn't going to be able to find it.

"I give up. Let's get the front door fixed."

Jake shrugged. "Okay, but I'm not at all sure that I can fix that lock."

"Well, we have to secure it some way," I said.

"There's a back door, isn't there? We can screw the front door shut for now and go in and out through the back until we can get it fixed properly."

"That's fine with me," I said.

"Do you want to come home with me so I can get some things I need to close the door properly?" Jake asked.

"Thanks, but if it's all the same to you, I'm going to stay here and keep looking around."

"What happened to us sticking together?" he asked me with a smile.

"What can I say? I made an executive decision."

"Okay, but be careful, all right?"

I grinned at him. "You said it yourself; nobody's coming back. They either found what they were looking for, or they broke in and realized that the files weren't here anymore."

"Just be careful. It took me a long time to find you, and I'd hate to have to start looking again."

"I'd hate that, too," I said.

After my husband was gone, I started taking a closer look around the office. Maybe we'd all missed something up until now.

At the very least, I was going to spend the next five or ten minutes hunting for it.

The search was still a bust, but I did manage to clean the place up a little. I took the trash I'd gathered out back, and as I tossed it into the bin behind the building, I noticed a few rose petals in the bottom of the can. What was going on here? I reached in and plucked two of them out, and then I wrapped them in my handkerchief. When Jake and I had interviewed Becky earlier, the only florist in town had told us that roses had been out of stock for at least a week. So where had all of these petals come from? Then I glanced over at Bobby Wells's trailer and saw his greenhouse.

That sparked something in my memory.

The florist might be out of roses, but I knew someone who had them.

I was walking toward Bobby's trailer when Jake pulled up.

"Going somewhere?" he asked me.

I got in and said, "Drive us over to Bobby's place."

"What are we looking for?"

"You'll see," I said.

We got to the trailer, and Jake headed straight for the front door, while I veered off so I could go into the little greenhouse set up nearby.

"Suzanne, what's going on?" Jake asked me from the door.

"I want to see something before you knock," I said as I pulled the door open and walked in. I bent down in the red clay dirt and studied the bushes inside; sure enough, it appeared that one of them had fresh cuts on a few of the stems. The flowers still there were all tight buds, but once they were cut, I knew it wouldn't take long for them to open up.

I'd found the source of the roses and, in the process, possibly the killer, too.

"What is it?" Jake asked.

"I found more petals in the trashcan out in back of the office," I said. "Becky told us that they were out of roses when we spoke with her, though. Then I remembered this little greenhouse. Unless I miss my guess, Bobby Wells was the one who was leaving single red roses around town for Teresa."

"That's good detective work, but it doesn't necessarily mean that Bobby killed Teresa Logan, even if he did leave her the flowers. You know that, don't you?"

"Yes, but both of the flowers we found were tossed in the trash. If he delivered those flowers and then saw that they'd been ravaged, couldn't that spur an act of violence after such vehement rejections from Teresa?"

"It's entirely possible," Jake said. "Let's see what he has to say for himself." My husband and I left the greenhouse and walked up to the trailer door, where he began to pound on it soundly.

There was no reply.

"Maybe he's at work," Jake said.

"He got fired, remember?" I asked.

"It sounds as though it was a rash decision to let him go. The manager could have changed his mind. Where else are we going to look for him?"

"You're right. It's not a great idea, but it's the best one we've got at the moment."

"No, Bobby missed his shift today," the manager said after we asked about the young man. "He's probably still angry with me for firing him the other day. After I cooled off, I called him and told him that he could come back in today, but evidently he's still upset about what happened. Still, he said he was coming back in, but he's not here, and that's really not like him. He's usually really prompt. It can't be his transportation, either, because I know for a fact that he just got his car back from the shop, and it's running fine, at least for now. Now I have to call someone else in to work his hours. Kids, right?"

Jake just shrugged in response, and we walked back out to the Jeep. "Where do we look for him now?" I asked him.

"The plain and simple truth is that we don't," my husband said. "We just don't have the resources."

"But we know someone who does," I said. "Should we tell Chief Grant what we discovered?"

"I don't see what it could hurt," Jake said. He dialed the chief's number and then killed the call. "It went straight to voicemail."

"Why didn't you leave him a message?" I asked.

"I wasn't exactly sure what I should say," he admitted. "Let's go talk to Joe and Becky, and then we'll try him again. I'd like to talk with both of them about these roses that keep showing up."

"I'm pretty sure they came from Bobby Wells," I said.

"I think so, too, but at least this gives us an opening so we can start asking new questions. We were looking for a new reason to talk to them both, and now we have one. The flower question is just a way to get our feet in the door. After that, we start pressing each of them harder about Teresa and see if either one of them cracks."

"Swing by the office first so we can take care of that door," I said. "While we're there, remind me to lock the back up. I forgot to lock that door in my hurry to get over to check out Bobby's rosebushes."

When we got there, someone was waiting for us, though.

"I've been looking all over town for the two of you," Alexander Rose said as we walked up to the front door of my building, which clearly showed signs of the earlier break-in. "Did you know that someone broke into this place?"

"We're aware of it," I said.

"What brings you by, Mr. Rose?" Jake asked him.

"I wanted to get inside to look for something that belongs to me," he said, and then he looked squarely at me. "Suzanne, I understand you own this building. You just keep popping up wherever I go, don't you?"

"I'm afraid I can't let you in here any more than I could back at Teresa's rental house," I said.

The young attorney sighed heavily before he spoke. "I'm afraid I owe you both an apology for earlier. I should have handled that much better than I did. My only excuse is that I'm so upset about what happened to Teresa that I'm not myself."

"What exactly is it that you're looking for?" I asked him. "Maybe we can help you if you trust us."

"Suzanne, may I have a moment?" Jake asked me.

"In a second," I said, a response that didn't please my husband very much. I turned back to the young attorney. "Well?"

"I don't suppose it will hurt to tell you. I gave Teresa a locket when we were dating, something of very little intrinsic value but that meant a great deal to me. It was my mother's, and I was fine with Teresa having it as long as there was any hope of us ever getting back together, but now that she's gone, I'd understandably like it back. That's why I wanted to see if Teresa had stored it at home. When you thwarted me there, I drove around a little, and then I went back to the house to speak with you again. If you were gone, I was hoping to find someone else there who might be a little more sympathetic to my cause. I was in luck. There was a woman and a police officer there when I arrived, and when I described the locket to them, they both promised to look for it as they worked. I was happy to wait there on the off chance that they found it, but the officer suggested I try here, just in case the locket was at her workplace instead of her home. Trish, was that the woman's name? She took my number and promised to call me if it turned up there. So you see, my quest is perfectly innocent."

"Why didn't you just come right out and tell us that earlier?" I asked him.

"As I said before, you caught me off guard." Alexander Rose's cell phone rang, and as he answered it, I turned to look at Jake, who only shrugged in response. The attorney's face broke into a smile over something the caller must have told him. "Never mind. Trish just found it."

"May I speak with her for one second?" I asked as I held out my hand for his cell phone.

He was so surprised by my request that he did as I'd asked without question. "Hey, Trish. It's Suzanne."

"Hi, Suzanne. What are you doing with Alex Rose? Does Jake know you two are together?"

"He's standing right here beside me," I said. "Could you describe what you just found to me?"

"Sure. It's an old locket with a T inscribed on the front of it. Let's see, it's about the size of a quarter, and it looks to be gold, but I'm guessing it's a pretty low grade. You'd think it would be worth a fortune given the way Alex Rose was carrying on about it, but if it's worth more than fifty bucks, I'll eat it."

So that much of his story checked out. "Can you tell me anything else about it? Does it open up?"

"Let's see," she said. After a full minute, she answered, "I had a devil of a time getting the thing open. There's a photo inside, and another engraving. I might be wrong, but I'd swear there's a picture of Alex when he was a boy inside."

"What's the engraving say?"

Almost at the same time, Alexander Rose and Trish spoke the words together. "To Mommy. I love you bunches. A."

"Thanks, Trish. Are you going to turn it over to him?"

"I would, but the chief needs to see it first. Do me a favor and tell him that he can pick it up at Chief Grant's office in an hour, would you?"

"Will do. And thanks. How are you holding up?"

"I'm managing," she said softly.

"Would you like me to come by and give you a hand? If nothing else, I can offer loads of moral support," I offered. I knew that Jake and I were in the middle of an investigation, but some things were more important than even that, like my friendship with Trish.

"No, I'm fine. Thanks for the offer, but with two of us already inside, I'm not sure this place will hold anyone else. Bye."

"Bye," I said, and then I handed the phone back to the attorney. "You can pick it up at the chief's office in an hour if he's willing to release it."

"Why wouldn't he be? I didn't kill Teresa. I couldn't have."

"Why not?" Jake asked him.

"I was at a conference in Columbia, South Carolina, at the time," he said. "I didn't even find out about Teresa until I got back to my office in Charlotte."

"Can anyone testify to that?" I asked him.

The attorney frowned. "I can provide an alibi, if it comes to that."

"For the entire night?" Jake pressed him.

"Yes, for the entire night," he said. Was he actually blushing? I had a hunch what that meant.

"You were really trying to get Teresa back, weren't you?" I asked. "Just not enough to pass up a little female company when you had the opportunity."

"Teresa made it clear that we were through, and I was vulnerable," he protested.

"I just bet you were."

"Honestly, I don't even know why I'm still standing here."

"Don't ask me. We're not keeping you," Jake said.

Before he could go, I called out, "Did you give Teresa any roses lately?"

"No, of course not. She thought it was a stupid waste of money, so I never would have done it. Why do you ask?"

"Just curious, I guess," I said.

Alexander Rose shook his head as he got into his car and drove away.

"Can you believe that guy?" I asked my husband after the attorney was gone. "He claimed to be trying to get back with Teresa, and all the while he's fooling around with somebody else. I feel sorry for her."

"I do, too, but knowing what we know about the man, I can't say that I'm all that surprised."

"Men are such dogs," I said angrily.

Jake shrugged before he spoke. "I'll grant you the fact that some men are, some of the time, but don't paint all of us with that particular brush. Remember, that description fits some women as well."

I nodded and kissed my husband soundly. "I know. You're right. Thanks for reminding me of that."

"That's just one of the many reasons that I'm here," Jake said with a grin.

"So, do we buy his story?" I asked him as we walked through the shattered doorframe and Jake got to work securing it.

"We need to tell the chief, but I don't see any reason that we shouldn't believe him. It's just too easy to disprove, and he may be a great many things, but he doesn't appear to be stupid."

"So we mark his name off our list until we learn otherwise. That leaves us with Joe, Becky, and the missing teen, Bobby Wells."

"Since we can't find Bobby at the moment, let's go speak with Joe Chastain again. How do you think he's going to feel about us showing up at his work again unannounced?"

"I'm guessing that he's not going to be happy to see us," I answered with a smile.

"I'm going to have to learn to live with the disappointment. How about you?"

"I'll find a way to cope," I said.

"There, that should hold for now," Jake said as he backed up and examined his work. It would take a wrecking ball to get through there now.

"It looks great. Let's go out the back, and we can get started investigating again."

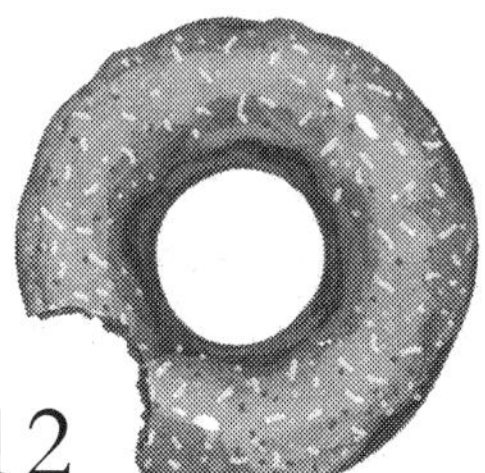

CHAPTER 12

"YOU TWO BACK AGAIN?" JOE Chastain said with a chuckle as we walked into the shop. I couldn't believe my eyes. The man actually looked as though he didn't want to kill us both this time.

"We thought we'd touch base with you again," Jake said, clearly as surprised by the man's reaction as I was.

"You got lucky. I'm just going on break," he said. "Come on. Let's go in back of the shop. I'm having a bite to eat, but there's not enough to share. Sorry about that."

"How about if we just keep you company?" I suggested. I noticed a faded tattoo on his arm. "Is that a rose, by any chance?"

"Nope, it was supposed to be a heart, but the guy that gave it to me had palsy or something. I thought the deal I was getting was too good to be true."

I couldn't imagine shopping for a bargain on permanent body art, and I wondered if he'd been drunk when he'd gotten it. "How do you feel about flowers?"

"I like 'em okay, I guess, but not enough to get a tattoo of one. Why do you ask?"

"Did you ever bring Teresa Logan roses?" I asked him.

He looked at me oddly, and then he started to laugh. "I can't say that it ever crossed my mind to bring my lawyer flowers, but I'll tell you one thing. If she were alive right now, I'd take her as many as I could carry."

"Why's that?" Jake asked him.

"Because she got me off the hook, just like she said she was going to!" he hooted as he took a bite of a sandwich he'd brought with him. "Can you believe it? The night she died, she told me she had something in the works and that I was probably going to be able to duck the charges, and sure enough, I got the call today. They're dropping everything against me. It turns out the guy I got into a disagreement with decided not to push it after all, and without their only witness, they don't have squat on me." Jake and I both must have looked surprised by the disclosure, because he quickly added, "I know what you're thinking, but I didn't say a word to him. I know intimidating a witness carries a lot of big-time consequences with it. The beauty of it was that I didn't have to do a thing. It turns out that he owes a ton of back child support money, and Teresa told him that if he went after me, she'd go after him and make sure that he paid every dime of it. If she was standing right here in front of me here and now, I'd have kissed her."

"Maybe your adversary killed her instead," I suggested halfheartedly. I'd been hoping that Joe had done it, not because of what he did for a living or even how he acted but because I thought he was a real menace when he drank, and I had a feeling that he was going to be celebrating with a bottle tonight, no doubt getting into more trouble again.

"Naw, they had their little conversation over the phone. He lives at the beach, and she called him down there to threaten him before he came up today to press formal charges against me. That woman was as good as her word. She told me she was going to make it happen, and I'll be dipped in tar if she didn't. It's a shame something happened to her. I haven't touched a drop of liquor since it happened, but tonight I'm going to make an exception, and I'm going to drink a beer in her honor. Who knows, maybe I'll have three or four," he said with a grin. "You two want to join me?"

"No, thanks. You know, you could always just send flowers

to the funeral," I said. The last thing this man should be doing was drinking, based on his history.

"What is it with you and flowers? I said I didn't care that much for them. Anyway, my break's about over. I can't tell you how good it feels not having that over my head anymore."

"Does the police chief know about it?" I asked as we started to leave.

"I wouldn't doubt it for a second," Joe said, and then he went back inside.

"It sounds as though Teresa helped him rather than hurt him, so he wouldn't have any reason to kill her, especially not after she got him off," I said as we made our way back to my Jeep.

"Can we believe him?" Jake asked me.

"I don't see why not. I'm going to call Chief Grant."

"To tell him what we've found out?" Jake asked.

"Yes, but also to warn him to be on the lookout for Joe Chastain tonight. I've got a hunch he's going to be in trouble again sooner rather than later."

"I'm just glad that he's not our headache anymore."

"And then there were two," I said.

"If we even have the killer on our list," Jake reminded me. "It might not be Bobby *or* Becky."

"I know that's a possibility, but if I were betting on it, I'd say that it was one or the other of them. Bobby could have easily lashed out at Teresa when she rejected him, and Becky has shown tendencies to display sudden bursts of anger. If Teresa met with her despite what she told us, and she said something to Becky that sparked her rage, she could have killed her on the spot. The truth is that either motive seems a bit feeble to me."

"Who knows what sets someone else off," Jake said. "I've seen far worse things done for much less reason."

"Worse than murder?" I asked, wondering what dark things my husband had dealt with while working as a state police investigator.

"You don't want to know," he said grimly, and I agreed with him a thousand percent.

"Should we see if Bobby's made it back home yet?" I asked him.

"If it's all the same to you, I'd rather take another run at Becky," he said.

"We might as well." Something had been weighing heavily on my mind, so I decided to just go ahead and say it. "You do realize at some point that I'm going to need to speak with my mother again, don't you?"

"Is she even in town? I thought she was joining Phillip right away."

"The last I heard she was still at home. You know what? I've already tried to tell her how I felt. It's time I talked to her spouse. Phillip is the one I should be talking to."

"While you're doing that, I want to ask the chief something," Jake said.

I pulled over and got out so Jake's conversation with the police chief wouldn't interfere with mine with my stepfather.

I needn't have bothered. I got Phillip's voicemail, and as soon as I got the prompt, I said, "Phillip, you need to call me as soon as you get this. We need to talk."

After I hung up and rejoined Jake, I asked, "What did you want to talk to him about?"

"I was wondering if he gave Rose back that necklace. If he did, it means that he doesn't think he's a viable suspect anymore, either."

I knew my husband was doing everything in his power to help the young chief, so I kept my mouth shut as I started driving toward the flower shop. Once Alexander Rose's and Joe Chastain's alibis were confirmed, we'd be able to narrow in on our last two suspects once and for all. If the police chief had anyone else in mind, he hadn't shared it with us. Were we missing something? I didn't know, and there was no way to tell, so all Jake and I could do was to press on and see if we could make one of them crack.

If we could find Bobby Wells, that was.

As it was, Becky Rusch was going to be getting our undivided attention next, whether she liked it or not.

"I'm sorry, but she went home sick forty-five minutes ago," the young girl behind the counter told us when we asked about Becky. Her name tag read CINDY, so I knew she must be the boss's daughter.

"What happened to her?"

"Some young guy I've seen working at the grocery store came by an hour ago and started arguing with her about roses. Is it our fault that we don't have any in stock? She told him to leave, but he wouldn't do it. Finally, she called me up front and told me to call the police. When I took my phone out, he left, but he wasn't very happy about it. I asked her if I should go ahead and call them, but she told me not to bother. Two minutes later she said that she had a migraine and that she was leaving. I've never been here by myself before. I'm going to call Mom and have her come by, but she's not going to be very happy about it. Sarah gets a little crazy sometimes when things aren't perfect here."

"Do you really call your mother by her first name?" I asked her. I'd known Sarah a long time, but I hadn't had too many encounters with her daughter.

"She likes me to do it when I'm at work, but sometimes I forget."

"Do you know where Becky lives?" Jake asked her.

"Sure, but I'm not supposed to give out that information."

"I'm the former chief of police," he said. "It's fine. You can trust me."

She nodded and said, "Okay, if you say so. Give me a second."

After Cindy disappeared in back, I said, "She didn't even ask to see your ID. Do you even know her?"

"No, but I'm guessing that she's just going to take my word for it. Let's give her the benefit of the doubt, shall we?"

"You're just saying that because she's a pretty girl," I pointed out.

"No, I'm saying it because she's young."

"Are you denying that she's pretty?" I asked him.

Jake laughed. "Oh, no. You're not going to get me to admit anything even remotely close to that."

"So you do think she's pretty," I said as I smiled at him.

"Maybe it's time to just stand here silently while we wait for her to come back."

"You know what? You're smarter than you look," I said, and then I kissed his cheek.

"I'd like to think so, and I certainly hope so," he said with a grin.

Cindy came back with a sticky note. "She just moved, so I wrote the address down for you."

"Where's she living now?" I asked.

"Mom, I mean Sarah, asked her if she'd stay at our place out by our greenhouses so she could be available in case the heater goes out or there's vandalism or anything like that. She's acting as kind of a caretaker out there."

"I hope she got a raise for doing it," I said.

"Her rent is basically free," Cindy said. "What more could she want?"

There was no point arguing with the boss's daughter.

"Thanks for this," Jake said as he plucked the note from her hand.

We drove out of town toward Maple Hollow, and as we did, Jake said, "You really don't mind if I notice whether a girl is pretty or not, do you?"

"Of course not. You can look all you want. It's the day you do more than that we're going to have a problem," I said happily.

"I'm married to the most beautiful woman in the world. Why would I jeopardize that?"

I had to laugh at that. "Nobody thinks I'm beautiful, but I know that some people consider me cute. I've learned to live with that."

"You're beautiful to me," he said. My husband wasn't one who was normally expressive like that, and I couldn't help but feel a warm glow inside.

"You know what? I think you're pretty peachy yourself," I said.

"I tell you that you're beautiful, and you compare me to a fruit?" he asked good-naturedly.

"Hey, I love peaches."

He laughed and then asked, "Do you want to know the thing I love most about you?"

"Sure. Why not?"

"You're fun to be with," he said.

I'd been expecting something a little grander. "That doesn't sound like much."

"Suzanne, it's everything as far as I'm concerned."

I thought about what he said before I spoke again. "It *is* important to enjoy yourself in a relationship, isn't it?"

"Absolutely."

We drove in silence for a few more minutes before I broke it. "I wish I could do it, but I can't stop thinking about Momma moving away from April Springs," I said.

"You should call Phillip back and get his take on it," Jake suggested.

"I tried while you were on the phone with the police chief, but he didn't pick up. I left a message, but he hasn't called me back, either."

"It will all work out for the best, one way or the other," Jake said, doing his best to reassure me. "You just have to have faith."

"Do you honestly believe that?"

"I don't know, but I'd like to," he said. "I meant what I said earlier. All you have to do is say the word, Suzanne, and I'll move anywhere in the world with you."

"I can't imagine ever leaving April Springs," I said. "It's always been home to me."

"There are other places out there that are just as nice," Jake said, "and you'd have your mother, too."

"That's the killer, isn't it? I'm taking you at your word, Jake. I'm not thinking about you, since you're willing to stay or to go. I love being near Momma, but will I still feel that way at the expense of giving up the donut shop and the cottage? This is where I work and live, and nearly all of my friends are here."

"I know you. You can make new friends wherever you go, but how much longer are you going to have your mother around?"

I took my eyes off the road for a second and glanced at him. "Jake, do you *want* to leave April Springs?" The thought had never even occurred to me.

"No, I didn't mean to give you that notion. It's just that my folks have been gone for a long time, and I'd give just about anything to watch a ball game with my dad or taste my mom's apple pie again."

"I get that, I really do, but I don't want to sell the shop and move, only to resent Momma later for forcing me into doing it."

"Suzanne, that's the beauty of the situation. You don't *have* to do anything."

"No, but if I don't, I lose my close contact with my mother.

If I decide to uproot us and move wherever they do, then I lose everything else."

"But me," he said.

"But you," I echoed.

We were fast approaching Becky's address, and I could see a row of four greenhouses coming up. There was a small bungalow in front, not much bigger than the place where Teresa Logan had been living, and there was an old car parked in front. A driveway full of gravel went from the road to the house, but not far beyond the edge of the drive, I could see the red dirt clay that was everywhere in our area.

"Let's go see what's going on with Becky," I said as I parked the Jeep in front.

"We can talk more about the situation with your mother later," Jake offered.

"Thanks, but if anything, it just confuses me more. For now, let's deal with something simple like Teresa Logan's murder."

"Do you call this simple?"

"No, but compared to my situation, it's practically cut and dried. All we have to do is figure out which one of our suspects killed her and then tell the police chief."

"Is that all?" Jake asked with a grin. "We should be done by nightfall, if that's the case."

"I know you're joking, but you might be right. I have a feeling that things are coming to a head sooner rather than later."

I knocked on the bungalow's door, but there was no response.

"Maybe she's in one of the greenhouses," Jake suggested.

"She had a migraine, at least according to Cindy," I answered, knocking harder this time but still not getting any response.

"Let me try," Jake said, and then he hit the door, banged on it, really, until I swore that I could see it shake in the frame.

Finally, the door opened. Becky stood there shielding her eyes. "What is it?" she asked softly.

"Sorry. We heard that you left work because of a headache."

"So your solution is to practically break my door down to get me to answer?" Becky asked testily.

"We won't keep you," Jake said. "Who did you have a fight with at the flower shop earlier?"

Becky shook her head instead of answering the question directly. "Cindy has a big mouth."

"We didn't realize that it was supposed to be a secret," I said. "Disgruntled customers are a liability in any business. I can't believe someone held you responsible for not having any roses in stock." We knew it had to be Bobby Wells, but what I wanted to see was if she were willing to admit it.

"Is that what she told you it was about?" Becky asked, looking around behind us for any signs that we might not have come alone. "You might as well come in. Just keep your voices down, okay?"

"We can do that," I promised in a gentler tone.

The place was kind of plain and ordinary inside, and I couldn't see a single personal touch that Becky had added to it. "How long have you been living here?"

"Not long," she admitted as she stepped into the darkened living room. Momma suffered from migraines on occasion, and I knew that light or even loud noises could bring on stabbing pain. I'd have to be careful and hope that Jake would modulate his voice as well. She added, "I came in and went straight to bed. Lying down in a dark room is the only way to combat these blasted things. Why are you two even here? What does it matter what happened to me earlier?"

"It matters to us. What happened with your customer earlier?" Jake asked her softly. "We wouldn't ask, but it's important."

"It wasn't a customer," she said. "It was Bobby Wells." So she'd decided to tell us the truth. That was one point in her favor. "A while back, he asked me for some advice about his roses. He's been growing some near his camper for a few years now, and he had some pests that needed addressing. I did what I could for him, and every now and then he came by for more advice."

"We heard that he was angry with you today," Jake prompted her.

"Angry? He was furious. He accused me of breaking into his greenhouse and stealing two of his roses! Can you imagine? He was yelling so loudly that I thought for sure Cindy must have already told you about it. I'm amazed people down the block didn't hear him."

"Why would he accuse you of that?"

"Who knows? The kid is off balance! He had this tragic crush on Teresa, and when she rejected him, he lost his mind! It wouldn't surprise me one bit if he's the one who killed her. You really should be talking to him."

"We've been trying to, but nobody can find him," I said. "Do you have any ideas where we might look?"

"No, I don't have the first clue," she answered. "After he came into the shop and yelled at me, he stormed out again. It triggered one of my migraines, so I left the shop and came straight here and went to bed. How did you find me? I didn't think anyone knew that I moved out here. Strike that. Cindy gave you my address, didn't she?"

I admitted as much. "Sorry. We were worried about you." That wasn't entirely the truth, but I was trying to get her sympathy. Bobby's behavior sounded as though he really was coming unraveled, but that didn't mean that Becky was completely off the hook just yet.

"I appreciate that, but I don't think he'll bother me anymore."

"Why do you say that?" Jake asked her.

"As he was exiting the shop, Bobby said that he was leaving the state and never coming back. It wouldn't surprise me if he was in Tennessee by now." She winced a little, and then added,

"I'm really sorry, but this headache isn't going to get any better until I lie down and put a cold washcloth on my face."

"Do you have any medicine for it?" I asked her.

"I've tried a few prescriptions, but nothing seems to help. Thanks anyway. Good luck."

"Thanks," I said. As I turned to go, I nearly tripped on a pair of boots by the door.

Becky leaned forward and grabbed them. "Sorry, I should have put them away when I got in, but my headache was so blinding, I could barely see a thing."

I brushed at my shoe and dislodged a bit of fresh red clay from it. "It's fine. I hope you feel better soon."

"All I need is some time alone," she said. "I'm sure that I will be."

Once we were outside and heading back toward the Jeep, Jake asked, "Do you believe her?"

"About Bobby? It sounded like him, didn't it? Plus, we have Cindy to vouch for Bobby's erratic behavior."

"Why would he accuse her of taking some of his roses?" Jake asked. "It doesn't make any sense. I've been working on the premise that Bobby left those flowers for Teresa. Could it be that we're missing someone else, another suspect that makes more sense than what we're left with?"

"I don't know," I admitted. "This case isn't nearly as simple as I first thought. I wonder if the police chief is having any more luck than we are."

"Maybe I should give him a call and ask," Jake suggested.

"Do you think he'd really tell you?" I asked him.

"Look at it this way. What can it hurt?" Jake's grin was infectious, and I hoped that he'd have more luck than I would if it were me making that particular call.

We got into the Jeep, and I pointed it back toward town as Jake made his call. As he waited for Chief Grant to pick up, I had a feeling in my gut that we'd missed something vital.

Maybe I wasn't nearly as good at this as I thought.

"He can't tell us anything officially," Jake said as he hung up.

"No surprise," I said.

"But he asked me for a favor," Jake continued.

"What does he need?"

"He's got his reasons, which he hasn't shared with me, but he thinks Bobby Wells holds the key to this case."

"I don't disagree with him on that, do you?"

"No, probably not," Jake answered. "He doesn't think he's running yet, though."

"Why not? Becky just made a pretty compelling case that he's leaving town as quickly as he can manage it."

"One of the chief's people found Bobby's vehicle in the bushes off Viewmont Avenue. It appears that he tried to cover it up with some branches, but it was spotted anyway."

"So, he can't leave town without his main source of transportation. That still doesn't explain why he'd come back to his trailer."

"His car might not be working, but he's got a motorcycle stored in a shed just off the property, and Chief Grant thinks that he's going to come back for it sooner or later. It's as good as any theory we've been able to come up with ourselves."

"Where do you come in?" I asked him.

"He wants some company on his stakeout," Jake admitted.

"Isn't it going to get crowded with all three of us in his squad car?"

"I'm sorry. I should have made myself clearer. The invitation was just for me."

"I know that, you goofball," I said with a laugh. "I was just teasing you. Sure, go on. I'll be fine on my own."

"What are you going to do? I might be awhile."

"I don't know. I'm a big girl; I'm sure I can come up with something."

"So I can tell him that it's okay?"

"You officially have my blessing," I said. "Are we eating dinner first?"

"He grabbed something from the Boxcar for the both of us," Jake admitted.

"Got it. Should I drop you off at Bobby's place or the police station?"

"Are you sure you're all right with this?" Jake asked.

"I'm fine," I said, and I meant it. "To be honest with you, I wouldn't mind having a little time alone. As much as I appreciate your offer, I'm not sure that I'm ready to pack up everything and move to the beach just because that's where my momma's going, you know? I always thought of us as mountain people, not beach folks."

"Why can't we be both?" Jake asked. "It's not like we'll never come back here to visit."

"I know, but it won't be the same, and you know it."

We got to the station, and I found the chief waiting for Jake. He had three bags with him, and he handed one to me. "I got you a burger, too," he said.

I laughed. "It's not because you feel guilty about pulling my husband away on the spur of the moment, is it?"

"Maybe," he confessed. "Does that mean you don't want it?"

"No, I wouldn't want to be rude," I said as I took the offering. "Now you boys behave yourselves, and don't stay out too late. Tomorrow's a school day."

They looked at each other and then at me without comment.

Oh, well. At least I thought I was funny.

"See you later," Jake said.

I waited until after they drove off, and then I drove the Jeep over and parked in front of the donut shop. The place was dark and empty inside, but it still felt like home to me. As I ate the burger and fries, I marveled at how Donut Hearts had become such a big part of my life. Could I walk away from it, just like that? Sure, I'd have Momma and Jake with me, but I'd be leaving behind the shop and, more importantly, a great many people I cared about, from Grace to Trish to Emily to George to dozens more folks that brightened my life on a daily basis merely by being in it.

I wasn't at all sure that I could do it, but then I thought about what Jake had said. Momma wasn't getting any younger—for that matter, neither was I—and I had no idea how much time I had left with her. Could I just let her leave my world completely, spending a few days with her every year and trying to cram a lot of living into a short amount of time? I finished the meal and started driving around randomly, trying to find the answer.

To my surprise, a little later I found myself on the road that led to Becky Rusch's place and those greenhouses. There was something that had been nagging at the back of my mind, but I hadn't been able to put my finger on it. Then it hit me. When I'd brushed up against her boot earlier, a bit of damp clay had gotten on my shoe, but she'd claimed to have come straight home from work and gone right to bed. So where did she get the fresh soil on her? Not on the walkway from the parking area. I'd seen that gravel myself. No, the only place she could have picked it up so fresh had to be from one of the greenhouses on the property. Had she just neglected to mention that to us, or had she deliberately lied about what she'd done when she'd gotten home? I decided to go ask her about it since I was so close by.

Her car wasn't there, though.

Evidently her migraine had suddenly improved.

But I still wanted to check on those greenhouses. I pulled my Jeep off to one side, grabbed a heavy-duty flashlight I kept beside me, and started toward the first structure. The gravel quickly ended, and I found myself walking in the same dirt as Becky's boots had been spattered with, moist red clay soil. What had been so important inside for her to hurry home after having a confrontation with Bobby Wells at the flower shop? The greenhouses had locks on the doors, but someone had accidently left the first one unlocked.

I walked in and looked around, turning my flashlight on and playing it around the space. It was starting to get dark out, and the greenhouse just accentuated that fact. At first I didn't see anything out of the ordinary, but then I flashed my light down on the one of the raised bed sections that was currently devoid of any plant life.

The soil there was freshly turned, but only in one small section, about six feet of the fifty-foot-long bed.

For the life of me, it looked like a grave.

It couldn't be that, though. Where was a shovel or even a hoe? There weren't any tools that I could see, and I couldn't stand the thought of not knowing if something, or someone, had been newly buried there. Getting down on my hands and knees, I started pulling away the loose soil on top.

When I got to a man's flannel shirt, I felt myself go numb.

It was the same pattern Bobby Wells had been wearing the last time I'd seen him alive.

I'd just found the missing clerk, and what was more, I finally knew who the killer was.

The only question was if I'd get help in time to do something about it.

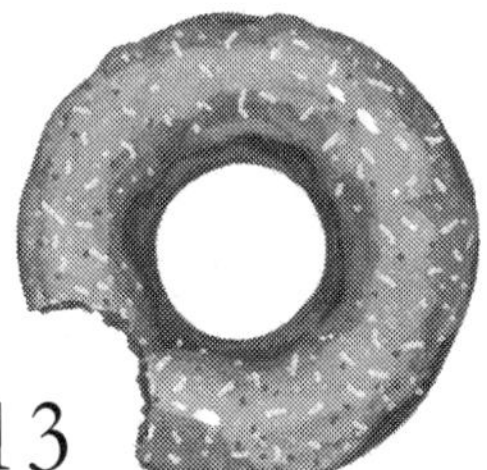

CHAPTER 13

"JAKE, I NEED YOU," I said as my husband's phone went straight to voicemail. Why did he never answer when I truly needed him? I called Chief Grant and got the same result. Maybe one of them would get my message, but I wasn't counting on it. I started for the door, dialing 911 along the way, when I saw headlights approach. They lit up the greenhouse! I'd stood up automatically in horror upon finding Bobby's body, and I had to wonder if I'd been outlined in the car's beams as it had pulled in. Ducking down, most likely too late, I punched the last "one" and finally got a real person on the other end.

Becky was too quick for me, though. She must have spotted my car the moment she'd driven up, and I'd probably given myself away in her headlights. I had a choice: I could finish the call, or I could defend myself. I threw my phone away from me into the darkness, hoping that whoever was on the other end would hear enough to put it together in time. I had other, more immediate problems on my mind. All I had with me was my heavy-duty flashlight, and I was going to use it. There was no place I could run to or anything I could hide behind, either. Standing by the door, I held the flashlight over my head, ready to strike, as Becky came in.

Unfortunately, she wasn't unarmed.

She'd picked up an ax on her way to me, and since it clearly trumped my flashlight, I did the only thing I could think of doing.

I threw it at her head with everything I had.

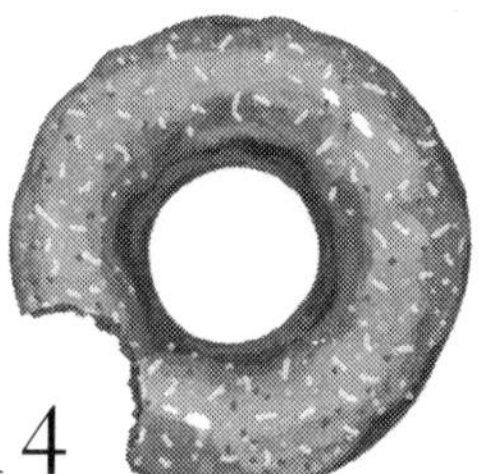

CHAPTER 14

UNFORTUNATELY, I MISSED.

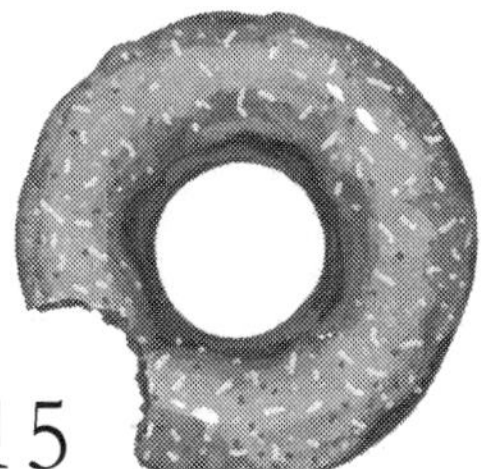

CHAPTER 15

Becky frowned at me as the flashlight hit the side of the greenhouse and fell to the ground, the beam of light still working, though shining in a very limited area now.

"That wasn't very nice of you, Suzanne." It was getting quite dark now, but Becky knew this place, and I didn't. She reached out and flipped an overhead switch that I'd missed before, bathing the place in gentle illumination.

"What did you expect me to do, stand there and let you clobber me with that ax?"

"Why not? It worked out fine that way with Bobby," she said with an uncharacteristic giggle. This woman had clearly gone over the edge. "You really should have minded your own business."

"Did Bobby know that you were the one who killed Teresa Logan? Was that why you killed him and buried him out here in one of the greenhouses?" I was trying to give the police operator a clue as to where we were, but I wasn't even sure that the call was active. Still, I had to act as though it was.

"Why are you talking like you're in some kind of play?" She looked around, and unfortunately, my cell phone was easy to spot. With a broad smile, she took the ax and slammed it down into my phone, neatly impaling it on the blade and holding it aloft like some kind of trophy. As Becky pulled it loose, I thought about trying to jump her, but she was too quick for me. "I don't think so." She looked around, and I did, too, hoping to find some weapon I could use against her, but the place was bare. "I used a shovel for Bobby, but I don't trust you. Get down on your hands and knees and start digging."

"Are you seriously asking me to dig him up?" I asked her, horrified by the thought of what I'd find if I did as she instructed.

"No, silly, move down a few feet. This is only temporary. Once things settle down, I'll move you both to a nice quiet spot I've already picked out in the woods. It's really quite lovely."

She was definitely insane. "You don't want to do this, Becky."

"Of course I do," she said, and then she gestured toward me with the ax.

It appeared that I had two choices: I could die, or I could dig.

I decided to dig.

But as I started moving the soil around enough to make my own shallow grave, I wanted some answers. I might be about to die, but I didn't want to go without being satisfied. "Why did you kill Teresa in the first place?"

"I met her at her office—oops, I lied to you about that, sorry—and she told me that she was dropping my case. She said that it was unwinnable, that I was unstable, and that she didn't want to have anything to do with me. I lost it; I admit it. A switch goes off in my brain when somebody calls me crazy! She turned to get my file for me, and I grabbed the closest thing I could find, a pine cone bookend, and I hit her with it. After that, I panicked! Wouldn't you? I ran out of there without even grabbing my file, which was probably a good idea, now that I think about it. The chief might have noticed if it was missing, since I already had an appointment on the books. I came back here and stewed over it, trying to come up with something to save myself, but I couldn't do it. Then I remembered Bobby's crush on her and the way she'd rejected him so soundly. I was at the grocery store when it happened, so why not use it to my advantage? I went by his trailer and cut a pair of his roses in the middle of the night, and then I took one to Teresa's rental house. I beat that thing silly, and then I dropped it out back. Why didn't the police find it?"

"Someone must have picked up the trashcan and put it over the stem by accident," I said as I paused in my digging.

She gestured with the ax again, which was all of the incentive I needed.

I kept digging.

"Why the rose at her office, then?"

"I wanted to make sure that the police got the message when they didn't find the first one," she said. "I'm not so sure our new police chief is bright enough to lead the force."

I strongly disagreed with her, but I didn't think it was the proper time or place to argue the fact with her. "Why kill Bobby, then?"

"I didn't want to, any more than I want to kill you," Becky said, her voice whining as she said it. "When I saw that idiot out walking on Viewmont Avenue, I pulled over and picked him up. His car broke down again, so he was heading home to get his motorcycle. Can you believe he was actually stupid enough to get in the car with me? You'll never guess where he was going, though. He was headed for my place! Bobby accused me of killing Teresa, but I denied it. I lured him out here to show him a piece of 'evidence' I had against the real killer, and the young fool believed me. I told him it was buried in the soil where I knew it would be safe, and when he started digging to retrieve it, I took care of him." She recounted what had happened as though she were reporting the weather.

"You might be able to get away with killing Teresa, and maybe even Bobby, but how are you going to explain me away?" I asked as I dug deeper and deeper. To my horror, it was beginning to look exactly like what it was to become, a shallow grave for a nosy donut maker.

"What's to explain? I'll pretend to be as puzzled as everyone else. Who knows? Maybe I'll start a rumor that you and Bobby were having a secret affair, and you ran off together."

"My husband won't believe that, not for one second, and neither will my family and friends."

"You give them all too much credit, Suzanne. We're designed to believe the worst in people." She peered over from the other side of the raised bed and looked down. "Nicely done. That should be deep enough."

I tried to grab her then, knowing that it was my last chance, but the soft soil gave way, and I found myself slipping into the hole I'd just dug.

Becky laughed at the horrified look on my face as I lay with my back in the grave I'd just dug for myself. "Don't worry, Suzanne. It will all be over soon."

With that, she raised the ax above her head and began to swing it down toward me.

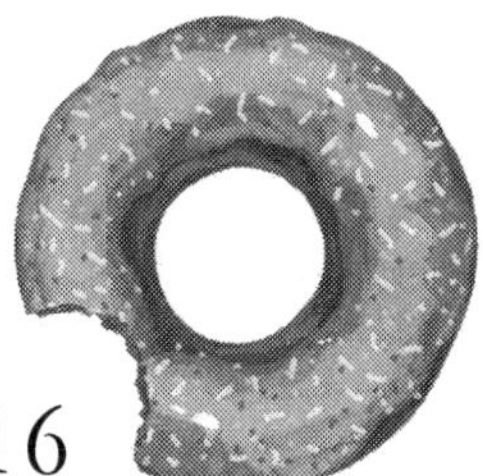

CHAPTER 16

That's when two shots rang out, spaced so closely together that they almost sounded as though they were echoes of each other instead of two separate reports.

As Becky's body fell toward me, I moved to one side to miss the falling ax.

They both landed solidly in the soil I'd pushed aside, and I shakily climbed out of the grave that had been meant for me.

CHAPTER 17

"SUZANNE, ARE YOU OKAY?" JAKE asked as he pulled me up to him.

"Don't. You're going to get dirty," I said. It was an odd thing to say, and I wondered if I might be in shock. Given the circumstances, it wouldn't have surprised me one bit.

"I don't care about that, you nit," he said as he stroked my hair. "That was brilliant of you."

"Which part, digging my own grave and almost getting killed or having to be rescued by the two of you?"

"You figured out what was going on before we did," Chief Grant said as he leaned down and checked for Becky's pulse. He shook his head, and I was surprised to realize that I felt nothing upon learning that my would-be assassin was now dead instead.

"I got lucky," I admitted, and then I started to shake. I'd been calm enough during the confrontation, but now I could barely stand up without Jake's support. Fortunately, I had it, in more ways than one.

"You followed your instincts," Chief Grant said. He looked down and saw Bobby's arm sticking out from the fresh soil and checked for a pulse there as well, though I could have told him that he was wasting his time. "Sorry it took us so long to get here."

"If I hadn't grabbed my phone to call you so I could tell you that it would be on silent, I never would have gotten your message in time," Jake said.

"But you did, and you got here right when I needed you." I looked around the greenhouse and felt as though I was going to be sick. "Can we get out of here?"

"Of course," Jake said. "An ambulance is on its way."

"They're wasting the trip," I said, fighting to keep myself from looking at the murderer and her final victim.

"It's for you," Jake said. "You're in shock right now."

"I must be," I said, and then, to my surprise, I fainted.

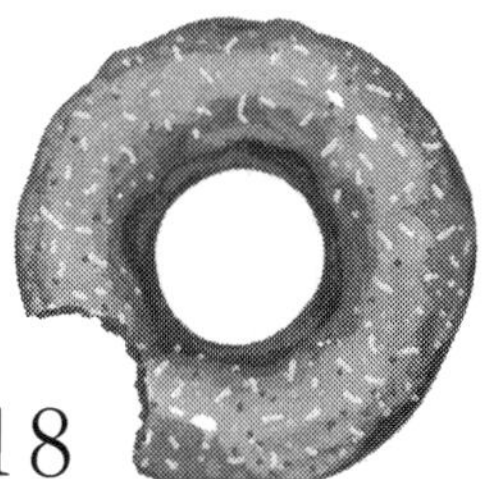

CHAPTER 18

"SUZANNE, ARE YOU OKAY?" I heard a familiar voice say from my bedside. It was my mother, and when I opened my eyes, I was happier to see her than I could have described.

"You're here," I said as I smiled at her.

"Where else would I be?" she asked.

"I don't know, maybe the beach," I said. "Could I have some water?" My throat was bone dry.

"Of course. I'll hold the cup for you," she said. "They gave you a straw earlier."

"No, I can get it," I said as she handed the cup to me. I noticed with surprise that my hands were pristine, though they'd been caked with soil the last time I'd seen them. "Somebody cleaned me up."

"They took good care of you," she said. "There's something we need to discuss. It's about the beach."

"Momma, I can't deal with that right now, not after everything that's happened."

"You're going to want to hear this. I'm not moving."

"Because of me? You can't do that," I protested as I looked around for my husband to back me up. "Where is Jake, anyway?"

"He went to get us some coffee," she said. "And I'm not staying because of you. Well, not entirely because of you," she amended.

"Is Phillip going by himself?" I asked. I couldn't bear the

thought that I might be the reason the two of them could be splitting up.

"No, of course not. He's my husband. He belongs with me."

"I don't understand," I said as I gently rubbed my head. Had I taken a blow to the skull that I didn't remember? No, there were no lumps or lacerations, at least as far as I could tell.

"It's all quite silly, really," Momma said. "We were watching a show on beach properties for sale. Phillip thought I was hinting that was where I wanted to live, and I thought he was doing the same. If we'd just discussed it without both of us running around like a pair of lunatics, we could have saved everyone a great deal of trouble."

"So you're not leaving me after all? I mean April Springs?" I asked her, feeling the relief flood through me as I realized that I wasn't going to have to leave, either.

"Of course not. I'll be here forever."

I knew that wasn't true, not about any of us, but I still appreciated the sentiment. I hadn't realized just how much tension I'd been holding in about the move until it was all gone. "I'm so glad."

"As am I," she said.

The door to my room opened, and Jake came in, carrying two cups of coffee. "Hey, you're awake. That's perfect, because I just heard that they're sending you home."

"Shouldn't she at least stay overnight for observation?" my mother asked, to no one's surprise.

"No, I want to be home with Jake," I insisted. "He can take care of me just as well as they can here."

"Better, if you ask me," Jake said with a grin. Momma frowned until Jake added, "You're welcome to join us at the cottage tonight, if you'd like. I know Phillip is driving back from the Outer Banks, but he won't be home until tomorrow. We have a spare bedroom, you know."

"I won't evict you from the master suite," Momma said.

Jake grinned. "I wasn't offering it. You can have Suzanne's room upstairs."

I was about to protest when Momma smiled. "And we're full circle. Yes, it's only fitting. I'd be delighted to accept your kind invitation."

"Good," Jake said, and then he leaned forward and kissed me. "Is that okay with you?"

"It couldn't be better," I said.

As the wheels of motion moved slowly discharging me so I could go home, I marveled at how much I nearly came to losing, and I promised myself to just smile the next time I was angry or frustrated with anyone I loved. Becky had lost much more than her temper when she'd struck Teresa Logan from behind, and while I didn't have the homicidal tendencies that she'd clearly been suppressing for years, I could find a way to stop taking minor inconveniences so seriously. If there was a lesson to be learned from all this, it was to value everything that I had, every second I was given to live, and I planned on doing it in earnest. I hadn't exactly taken my life for granted up to that point, but I vowed that I'd do my best to cherish it even more, especially after coming so close to losing it all.

RECIPES

Suzanne's Light and Airy Donuts

Let's start this section with an actual donut recipe, since I've found that I'm offering a great variety of other choices below. However, this *is* a donut mystery, so featuring at least one recipe isn't out of line. This donut is a little different. The basic dough takes longer to prepare, but it's worth it, at least according to my family. I've served this to guests, and commenters have compared them to beignets and funnel cakes, and while I can see the resemblance, I believe they offer a unique taste all their own. Be warned. This recipe took me quite a few times to produce consistently, so don't be discouraged if your first few attempts don't pan out.

Ingredients

- 2 packets active dry yeast
- 1¼ cups warm water
- 1¼ cups evaporated milk (buttermilk can be substituted if desired)
- ½ cup white granulated sugar
- 2 eggs, beaten
- ¼ teaspoon salt
- 5–6 cups bread flour
- ¼ cup canola oil

- ½ cup confectioner's sugar, if desired
- Enough canola oil to fry the dough

Directions

Dissolve the yeast in warm water, stir and then add evaporated milk, granulated sugar, the two beaten eggs, and the salt. Stir in about 2½ cups of flour until the mixture is smooth. Next, add the ¼ cup of oil and another 2 to 2½ cups of flour, stirring again until it's roughly incorporated. Next, flour a large surface and turn the dough out onto it. Work all of the flour lightly in and then put it into a greased bowl, cover, and chill for at least two hours. When you're ready, preheat the oil in your frying container to 360 degrees F. While you're waiting for it to come to the correct temperature, roll the dough out to approximately ¼ inch thick, and then cut out whatever shapes suit your fancy. We have cookie cutters in a variety of shapes, and we like to play with this dough. When the oil reaches the proper heat, drop your dough into the oil, being careful not to crowd the donuts as they cook. Fry these for 2 minutes for each side (or until golden brown), remove from the oil, drain for a few moments on dry paper towels, and then dust with powdered sugar and enjoy.

This recipe yield depends largely on the shapes you use cutting out the dough, but it's usually enough for four people.

So Far, My Best Stovetop Breakfast Frittata

In case you haven't been reading my Cast Iron Mysteries (and why wouldn't you? I'm a big fan of them myself, so pick one up and see if you like it!), you may have missed my family's latest fascination with frittatas. While these aren't donuts (clearly), some of you have been saying lately that you'd like to see some of the recipes offered in the back that are written about within the books, and I completely relate to your frustration. When the recipes have been offered in earlier books, I'll do my best not to repeat them, but when it's something new to the series, I'm going to feature them, with the understanding that I may not remember to do it or have room to every single time. I offered my initial frittata recipe awhile back in *Cast Iron Motive* (book #4 in the series), but I've been experimenting lately, and I've come up with a recipe I like even more than the first one. If you've been following my recipes all along, you'll know that I'm not a chef, nor do I claim to be a cookbook author (though I feel that way sometimes, sharing the meals I make with you all, my dear readers). I'm just a plain and simple home cook and baker, and I love tweaking old recipes and trying to make them better. Sometimes it results in complete and utter failure, but sometimes it's a roaring success. I like to think this one is in the latter category and not the former. The beauty of this recipe is that you don't need cast iron cookware to make it. Any nonstick or well-greased skillet with a lid will do nicely. Don't be fooled by the simplicity of this meal. This recipe is more than just glorified scrambled eggs, and it doesn't have to go under the broiler, either. All in all, I approve of simple ways when they work perfectly fine, so I urge you to try this one yourself. If you want to broil this anyway, it's perfectly fine with me. Just stop the cooking process a little earlier before you slide your oven-proof skillet under the broiler to give it a crisper and darker top.

Ingredients

- 6 large eggs, whisked well
- 1/4 teaspoon salt and pepper, or substitute your favorite seasoning
- Filling (total amount should equal approximately 1 cup)
- 2 ounces olive oil
- green bell pepper, diced
- greens mix (spinach, kale, and arugula is one we like) or just spinach, raw
- 3 cheeses, extra sharp cheddar (shredded), mozzarella (shredded), and feta, (which doesn't need to be shredded at all)
- prosciutto or bacon, diced or crumbled, as the case may be

Directions

Dice the bell pepper and sauté over medium heat in the olive oil for 5 minutes, then set it aside to cool.

Beat the eggs in a large mixing bowl then add the seasoning of your choice. I like simple salt and pepper, but if you have a seasoning blend you like, use that instead. Mix the seasoning in, then add 1 to 1½ cups from the fillings listed above (your preference) and stir this into the egg mixture. I feel all three cheeses add something to this dish, as well as the pepper and prosciutto. In my mind, it's the perfect blend of tastes, but by all means, use whatever you'd like, adding things liked sautéed mushrooms, ham, other cheeses. This is all about your taste and preference, not mine!

On the stovetop, heat your skillet somewhere between low to medium heat, then add the egg and filling mixture and cook for 5 to 7 minutes, stirring a few times initially, and then covering until the eggs are almost set. You can tell it's nearly ready when you shake the pan and the egg part of the mixture is mostly solid. There may be some liquids from the cheese, but you'll be able to tell the difference. Remove from heat and let it stand 5 to 10 minutes before serving. This will allow the meal to rest. It's going to be hard not to grab a fork and start eating out of the pan, and it's pretty good that way (don't ask me how I know that. I refuse to incriminate myself any further), but it's better if you wait.

Serves 3 to 5 people, depending on the size of the slices

Raisin And Oatmeal Delights

If you ask me, too many people give raisins a bad rap. I love them, fresh from the box or baked into a delicious treat, but if you're not a fan, this recipe will still be good without them. If you like dried cranberries instead, you could try those, but oatmeal alone is good, though not without the inherent sweetness of the added fruits. Sometimes I've been known to go a little crazy and start adding whatever kind of dried fruits I can find, so feel free to experiment. Some of my favorite recipes have been discovered that way, but in the spirit of full disclosure, some of my worst ones have come to life using that method, too. Hey, what's life in the kitchen without a little risk every now and then?

Ingredients

- ½ cup granulated white sugar
- 2 eggs, beaten
- ½ cup buttermilk (whole or 2% will also work)
- 2 tablespoons canola oil
- 1 teaspoon vanilla extract
- 2 cups bread flour or regular unbleached flour
- 1 teaspoon baking soda
- 2 teaspoons baking powder
- 1 teaspoon cinnamon
- 1 teaspoon nutmeg
- ¼ teaspoon salt
- 2 tablespoons oatmeal (old-fashioned, not quick oats)

Optional

- 1 tablespoon dried cranberries

- 1 tablespoon raisins
- 1 tablespoon other dried fruit (your choice)

Directions

Heat enough canola oil to 360 degrees F to fry your donuts. While the oil is heating, in a large mixing bowl, add the sugar slowly to the beaten eggs, then add the milk, 2 tablespoons of canola oil, and the vanilla, mixing it all in well. Then, in a separate bowl, sift together the flour, baking soda, baking powder, cinnamon, nutmeg, and salt. Add the oatmeal, mix lightly, and then add the dry fruit to the mix, lightly coating the pieces. This allows the fruits to keep from sinking into the bottom of the mix. Slowly add the dry ingredients to the wet, mixing thoroughly one more time. Rake the dough into the heated oil in tablespoon increments, cooking 2 minutes on each side, or until each donut is golden brown all the way around. Drain on a paper towel and coat lightly with confectioner's sugar or a simple glaze of water, vanilla, and confectioner's sugar.

This recipe makes from 12 to 16 donut rounds.

Momma's Pot Roast

In the spirit of full disclosure, I featured a variation of this recipe in *Bad Bites* (Donut Mystery #16), but I've been experimenting with the recipe lately, and I wanted to revisit it here. I make this in my crock pot (slow cooker to some of you), but sometimes I do it in my cast iron Dutch oven. When I share that particular variation with you, it will be included in the Cast Iron Cooking Mysteries, not here. My, that was a rather shameful plug for one of my other mystery series, wasn't it?

Anyway, a good pot roast is something my family loves any time of year. We dine on the roast and vegetables the first time around, and later, the leftover tender meat makes an excellent sandwich. I love mine on toast with olive oil mayonnaise, some pepper jack and mozzarella cheese, and some loose greens leftover from my frittata recipe above. Nothing goes to waste in my household! This is a delicious meal, and the prep work couldn't be much easier. The hardest part is being in the house for the 8 to 9 hours it takes to cook. The aromas are enough to drive anyone crazy!

Ingredients

- 1 potato, russet, cut into large sections
- 1 green bell pepper, cut into large sections
- 1 large onion, you guessed it, cut into large sections
- 8 medium carrots, peeled and cut into large sections
- 1 can beef broth (I use half, and then add 1/2 cup of water as well)
- 2 – to 2½-pound pot roast (I love a good beef tip roast, but I usually wait for it to go on sale!)
- salt and pepper

Optional (either of these adds a nice dose of flavor)

- 1 packet French Onion soup mix (powdered) or
- 1 packet beef stew dry mix for slow cooking

Directions

This one couldn't be easier. Prep the vegetables as noted above and add them to the bottom of a lined crock pot. I like to use the disposable clear bags to make cleaning up a cinch. After layering the potato, green bell pepper, onion, and carrots on the bottom, add the broth and water before adding the meat. If you use the onion soup mix or the beef stew mix, dissolve in ½ cup water in a small bowl and stir. Place the meat on top of the veggies, and then pour the mixture over the top of the meat. Cover and cook on low for 8 to 9 hours. There's no need to brown this meat, a step I personally love skipping! Resist the urge to lift the lid at any time. The steam does a great deal of the work in slow cooking, so you don't want to release that. Pull everything out and let it rest 5 to 10 minutes, then serve and enjoy.

Serves 4 to 7 people, depending on their appetites

If you enjoy Jessica Beck Mysteries and you would like to be notified when the next book is being released, please send your email address to newreleases@jessicabeckmysteries.net. Your email address will not be shared, sold, bartered, traded, broadcast, or disclosed in any way. There will be no spam from us, just a friendly reminder when the latest book is being released.

Also, be sure to visit our website at jessicabeckmysteries.net for valuable information about Jessica's books.

OTHER BOOKS BY JESSICA BECK

The Donut Mysteries
Glazed Murder
Fatally Frosted
Sinister Sprinkles
Evil Éclairs
Tragic Toppings
Killer Crullers
Drop Dead Chocolate
Powdered Peril
Illegally Iced
Deadly Donuts
Assault and Batter
Sweet Suspects
Deep Fried Homicide
Custard Crime
Lemon Larceny
Bad Bites
Old Fashioned Crooks
Dangerous Dough
Troubled Treats
Sugar Coated Sins
Criminal Crumbs
Vanilla Vices
Raspberry Revenge
Fugitive Filling

The Classic Diner Mysteries
A Chili Death
A Deadly Beef
A Killer Cake
A Baked Ham
A Bad Egg
A Real Pickle
A Burned Biscuit

The Ghost Cat Cozy Mysteries
Ghost Cat: Midnight Paws
Ghost Cat 2: Bid for Midnight

The Cast Iron Cooking Mysteries
Cast Iron Will

Cast Iron Conviction
Cast Iron Alibi
Cast Iron Motive

Made in the USA
San Bernardino, CA
04 May 2016